SCORED

GOLD HOCKEY #20

ELISE FABER

SCORED

BY ELISE FABER

Newsletter sign-up

Gold Hockey Series

Golden
Scored

Gold Cast of Characters

Heroes and Heroines:

Brit Plantain (Blocked) — first female goalie in the NHL, loves boy bands

Stefan Barie (Blocked) — captain of the Gold

Sara Jetty (Backhand) — artist and figure skater

Mike Stewart (Backhand) —defenseman for the Gold, romance guru

Blane Hart (Boarding) — center for the Gold, number 22

Mandy Shallows (Boarding) — trainer and physical therapist

Max Montgomery (Benched) — defensemen for the Gold, giant nerd

Angelica Shallows (Benched) — engineer at RoboTech, also a giant nerd

Blue Anderson (Breakaway) — top forward in the league and for the Gold

Anna Hayes (Breakaway) — Max's former nanny, no relation to Kevin Hayes

Rebecca Stravokraus (Breakout) — Gold publicist, makes killer brownies, known at PR-Rebecca

Kevin Hayes (Breakout) — forward for the Gold, no relation to Anna Hayes

Rebecca Hallbright (Checked) — nutritionist for the Gold, plethora of delicious vegan recipes, known as Nutrionist-Rebecca

Gabe Carter (Checked) — doctor, head trainer for the Gold

Calle Stevens (Coasting) — assistant coach for the Gold, former national team member

Coop Armstrong (Coasting) — talented forward on the Gold, addicted to historical romance audiobooks

Mia Caldwell (Centered) — 5th degree black belt, brings the snark

Liam Williamson (Centered) — Gold forward finding his love for the game, charming and pushy in equal measures

Charlotte Harris (Charging) — new Gold GM, hates losing and the game Chubby Bunny

Logan Walker (Charging) — defensemen for the Gold, skills include: cockiness and being able to buy presents that make Charlotte squirm

Dani Eastbrook (Caged) — video coach for the Gold, tech nerd, could fix your computer in a flash, shy

Ethan Korhonen (Caged) — forward for the Gold, killer power play skills, known as Big Juicy Brain

Fanny Douglas (Crashed) — silver medalist, skating coach for the Gold

Brandon Cunningham (Crashed) — brown curls, penchant for hallways, Kaydon Lewis's agent

Kaydon Lewis (Cycled)— yummy stubble, great with kids, doesn't mind a little snot

Scarlett Andrews (Cycled)—quiet, perfectionist, resembled Bambi on ice

Charlie Andrews (Caught)— Scarlett's brother and total romantic

Kacee (Caught)— the woman inside the giant Gold nugget

Joshua Webb (Cap)— tall, smart, and handsome, the newest captain of the Gold

Jess White (Cap)— assistant video coach and obsessed with a certain new captain

Benjamin Roberts (Covered)— snarky, smart, and dipping a toe where he shouldn't

Jordyn Webb (Covered)— single mom and Josh's sister

Will Johansson (Crushed)— smart, sensitive, and likes Shirley Temples

Lily Cartwright (Crushed)— sports psychologist and obsessed with fluffy pancakes

Additional Characters:

Bernard — head coach

Richie — equipment manager

Dan Plantain — Brit's brother

Diane Barie — Stefan's mom

Pierre Barie — Stefan's dad, owner of the Gold

Spence — former goalie, married to Monique, daughter Mirabel

Monique — married to Spence, former model

Mirabel — daughter of Spence and Monique

Mitch — Sara's boss

Allison and Sean — Blane's parents

Pascal — Devon Scott's security lead

Roger Shallows — Mandy's dad

Grant and Megan — Devon's parents

ONE

BRIT

My teammate's first game back after his life-changing injury was a huge success.

But the impromptu wedding at center ice meant that the game hadn't started on time.

Which meant that it hadn't *ended* on time either.

And I still had to do my post-game routine—making sure I keep up with my conditioning, my strength training.

My rehab.

And, honestly, I don't mind getting home late.

Roxie will already be asleep, so I won't miss out on time with my daughter.

It also means less time in an empty bed, staring at the ceiling and trying to figure out how I'd managed to so thoroughly fuck up my life.

Well, not *all* my life.

My daughter is awesome. The team is doing great. It's just—

Stefan—my husband—has been distant lately.

Cold and unreachable.

Well, honestly...

That distance has been around much longer than *lately*.

Empty beds. Not coming to the team's home games. Missing meals.

Just...distant.

And every time I try to talk to him about it, we end up in a fight. Me frustrated because he's not talking to me. Him frustrated because I'm pushing.

Sighing, I hit the button to close the garage door, waiting until it shuts completely before I unlock the door into the house and step inside.

Then pause as I wait for my eyes to adjust to the darkness.

No under-cabinet lights left on for me in the kitchen, their soft glow illuminating my walk down the hall, making sure I don't trip over a stray toy or shoe or jacket or mini hockey stick or ballet tutu or karate belt from my tiny crazy, wants-to-do-every-activity little human.

I don't have that now.

I may not ever have it again.

I sigh, hang up my coat, then toe off my shoes and shove them into the rack before padding into the kitchen.

Dark.

Quiet.

I need water, a snack, and then to sleep so I'll be rested enough to get up with my rambunctious kiddo.

Which will likely happen far too early tomorrow—er—*this* morning.

Stretching a hand across the wall, I hit the switch to turn on those under-cabinet lights.

Then gasp, clamping a hand to my throat.

Stefan is sitting on one of our barstools, elbows resting on the island. Silent. Staring at me. After having sat in the dark for who knows how long.

"Hey," I manage to push past my pounding pulse, my suddenly tight throat.

Where had the warmth in his eyes gone?

Had it just disappeared one day?

Or had it slowly, incrementally just faded away, slipping from his blue irises like grains of sand in an hourglass, so slowly that I hadn't noticed?

Not until that hourglass was empty.

Not until his eyes had transformed from Caribbean warm waters into...ice.

He doesn't reply—not to my gasp, not to my greeting. And he doesn't take me close, lips curving as he nuzzles my throat, drawing me against the warm, strong expanse of his chest, whispering a soft apology in my ear for startling me before complimenting me on the game.

Before taking me up to bed, exhausting me in other, more pleasurable ways.

And I don't know what to do, what to say to this man who's become a stranger by millimeters, so I...

Turn for the fridge, for the snack, for the chocolate milk I prefer to drink post game, the veggies I precut that are waiting for me. I'll dip them into some hummus, drink that chocolate milk, plenty of water, and call it a good enough recovery meal.

Our team's nutritionist, Rebecca, will be pleased.

After grabbing the container with sliced carrots and celery, a pepper, some kale, I spin back around.

Set it on the counter.

Pop open the top.

Go back for the hummus and slop in a couple of tablespoons.

Wash the spoon, slot it into the dishwasher. Rinse the lid.

All the while, my heart is pounding and I'm waiting, wishing, praying.

Because...this is wrong, and I don't know how to fix it.

Meanwhile, my husband just sits on that barstool, not in any hurry to break the silence, and neither am I, I suppose.

Because I'm a coward.

Because I've pushed and been rebuffed so many times that I'm scared to reach out again, scared to be burned again.

But...

It's the hard stuff that's worth doing.

Advice I'd given my former teammate, Rome, not long ago.

Advice that might be sound but is really fucking hard to do in actuality.

But...

I *have* to do it.

This is the love of my life. The man I've been with for more than a decade. The other half of my soul.

Isn't that worth risking a few burns?

Heart lurching, I open my mouth.

Then bite back whatever words I was about to say when my husband finally speaks.

And does it in a tone that's, unfortunately, become familiar.

Cold.

Sharp.

Resolute.

"I want a divorce."

Two

BRIT, SIX MONTHS LATER

I'm in hell.

Literal hell.

Staring at the beautiful brunette in front of me.

With kind eyes.

Who's...fucking my husband.

Ex-husband.

That addendum sends a pulse of pain shooting through the backs of my eyes, the shards of my broken heart digging into my soft tissue.

But they're familiar hurts.

Because, over the last year, they've *become* familiar.

More familiar than my ex's new girlfriend, Tiffany.

Yup.

Fucking *Tiffany*.

And worse, I can't even be upset.

Because she's *nice*.

"I was wondering if you would be all right with me taking Roxie to get our nails done?" Tiffany says, holding her hand up and showing off long acrylic nails that I could never get away with.

Because they won't fit in a goalie glove.

I wince.

"I won't get her fake nails, of course," she says quickly, wrongly reading the grimace I hadn't been able to keep inside—

Because I'm not that kind of woman, because I couldn't give Stefan that.

Because...maybe I wasn't woman enough for him.

I clench every muscle in my body—and there are a lot of them, and they're defined unlike the slender waif in front of me, and—

I hold back a shudder.

Enough.

Tiffany keeps talking. "...just some colored polish that she can pick out, and a hand massage—" She falters here, probably because my gaze is still locked on her fingers, staring at those sharply pointed nails and wondering how she can possibly get anything done with them.

Wondering if Stefan likes them digging into his back when he fucks her—

Pain lashes across my stomach sharply, perhaps even more sharply than nails like that can dish out.

It leaves an intense burn in its wake that spreads out and encompasses me from head to toe, stealing my words, leaving Tiffany to ramble.

"Or maybe just pink with a little sparkle?" she says. "Or nude? Or even clear. If you don't want her to have color."

My baby girl *loves* color and has sported her nails with all manner of pastel to bright to neon. But this woman wouldn't know that, would she?

Because she's new in our lives.

I press my tongue to the roof of my mouth, push out a silent breath through my nose.

And put my petty bitch to the side.

"I think Roxie would love going with you to get her nails done." I force my lips to curl up into a smile, know that anyone who truly knew me would see right through it. But I'm making the effort, okay? Even with my heart breaking into a thousand pieces inside my chest. "Just let me know when, and I'll make sure that she's there."

Even words. But I have the feeling that they don't completely hide the shards inside my chest, the ones that keep jabbing at me.

She reaches over and squeezes my arm, tone gentle when she murmurs, "Thank you."

Her touch is like ants crawling up my arm...

But I know that's me, not her.

I carefully pull free, force my mouth to remain in that facsimile approximation of a smile. "Of course," I say brightly. "I'm sure you two will have a great time." *Squeeze.* My lungs. *Jab.* My heart. "Now"—I incline my head toward the ice where Roxie and her team are finishing up practice and now skating for the exit —"if you'll excuse me, I'll get her changed and ready so you two can have some bonding time."

Tiff's face does something, and I realize that I've unknowingly touched on a sore spot, and it takes a heartbeat for me to collect my thoughts.

The petty bitch in me wants to exploit that vulnerability.

To poke at it.

To hurt her like she's hurting me.

Only...I'm divorced. She's not fucking my husband. Isn't the other woman—even if it feels like it.

She's just a nice person who's nice to my ex and nice to my daughter and—

I didn't get where I am by being a petty bitch who tears down innocent women.

I lift motherfuckers up like I've got Michelle Obama's arms, or maybe like one of those World's Strongest Woman's competitors, picking up a giant rock for no reason and slamming it down on top of a pedestal.

Look what I can do, bitches!

"Mom!"

I blink, realize I've been standing there, lost in my thoughts.

I shake myself, turn to Tiffany, smile again. "I'll get her changed and take the stinky gear home." More smiling. Because smiling is great. Smiling is everything. "That way we don't have to subject your car to the stench while you guys get your nails done."

"Really?"

But it's not Tiffany talking. I glance down, realize my little girl has come close enough to hear.

"I can get my nails done like Tiffany?" she exclaims, bouncing on the toes of her skates. Red-cheeked and sweaty, still clad head to toe like a little marshmallow in her hockey gear, and excited about a manicure.

I grin, and it's a real one this time.

"Yeah, baby," I tell her. "You can get your nails done like Tiffany."

She whoops.

"But we need to get you changed, and then you have to wash your hands"—because gloves are the stinkiest, no matter how hard I try to keep them smelling fresh—"and face"—because that's just a good habit—"but then, yes, you can go with Tiffany and get your nails did."

I draw out the last word, wiggling my fingers in her direction, and getting that little giggle from her that settles in my belly, my heart, my soul.

"Let's go, stinky," I tease, thumping her lightly on the top of her helmet and nodding at Tiffany. "Be out in a few."

Tiffany is bouncing slightly, her excitement about spending time with my daughter as palpable as Roxie's.

It hurts.

But I've always said that the more people around Roxie who love her, the better.

So, I go into the locker room. I help my daughter take off her gear. Walk her to the bathroom so she can wash her hands—and her face.

Then I send her off with Tiffany to get her nails done.

And my car is subjected to the stink of wet, dirty hockey gear the entire way home.

THREE

STEFAN

"As your lawyer, I would highly advise you don't agree with these terms," my attorney, Russ Laughlin, says, flipping through the thick-as-shit file on his desk and shaking his head.

Because...

Brit hired Bec Darden—

Or Bec Darden's firm, anyway, because Darden herself focuses on employment law, but as a partner in a nationally recognized law practice and a total shark, she has plenty of family law attorneys under her purview.

Including the one who's handling Brit's side of our divorce.

"Give her anything she wants," I mutter. "I just need to have fifty-fifty custody."

"She's not contesting the custody arrangements," Russ says, "the house, on the other hand—"

"She can have it."

"And the property up in Tahoe," he says, flipping the page on his legal pad. "I know you haven't started building yet, but it's worth—"

"She can have it."

"And—"

I glance up, meet his eyes, locking our stares, trying to make this man understand something he has absolutely no ability to comprehend. "She. Can. *Have*. It."

"Stefan—"

"Look, man," I say, pulling out my phone, glancing at the time. Roxie's got to be off the ice by now, and I want to make sure she and Tiffany are getting along okay.

That Brit—

The knife to my gut is almost immediate, jabbing home, yanking upward, exposing my insides to the world.

Or maybe that's just what all of the sports blogs and TikToks and social media posts on other platforms have done.

Worse than when we first started dating.

Worse because hockey royalty has fallen apart.

Because *I* hurt her.

Russ clears his throat and I shove that down, way fucking down, knowing that I had to do it. Knowing it was the only way. Knowing that—

It's all fucked up and twisted and even if I wanted to go back, I can't. Not now. Not when—

"Look," I say again, cutting that thought off and focusing on the present, on the man who's sitting behind his desk, working his ass off because Bec Darden's firm is making him pay for each and every filing with blood, sweat, and frustration. "I need to go. I don't give a fuck about the money or the house or the property. I want to be free of this, of *her*"—my gut clenches—"I'm ready to be done with it all. And...just give her what she wants," I mutter.

Russ has gone still, his eyes searching mine for a long moment.

Then he nods, sighs, and closes the file. "I get it, Stefan. I'll make it happen."

"Thanks," I say, pushing up to my feet, reaching over to shake his hand.

We exchange goodbyes, and my phone buzzes, telling me that Tiff and Roxie are getting their nails done. That, at least, has my lips twitching, amusement in my belly because Roxie is going to *love* that. And then I'm out into the hall, walking to my car, determined to put this shit of a divorce behind me.

I drive home, weaving through the typically awful Bay Area traffic.

And then I'm pulling into my driveway.

Unfortunately, it's not empty—even though Tiffany and Roxie are still at the nail salon.

Nope.

My mother's car is taking up most of it, and when I park at the curb and walk inside, I see she's taking up most of the space within the kitchen as well.

The delicious scent of her lasagna reaches my nose, her music fills the air, blasting against my eardrums, and—

Her mere presence has the ragged gash in my heart settling.

At least until I get a glimpse of her face.

Then I can barely resist holding in my beleaguered-teenage-boy-facing-his-disapproving-mother's groan.

I don't have time or patience for this shit.

Sighing, I hang my keys on the hook just inside the kitchen, start to turn for the bedroom. I want to change out of my adulting clothes, pull on some sweats, to brace for the tornado of energy that is my daughter.

But...

I don't get that far.

The music cuts off.

"What the hell are you doing, Stefan?"

I sigh, turn back, a throb beginning in my temple.

"The divorce," she says. "You're still really going through with it?"

"Considering we've had this conversation a dozen times over the last months, Mom, I think we both know the answer to that."

Her eyes flash in that distinctive *Mom* way, irritation and disappointment and love all jumbled up together. "Don't you take that tone with me," she says, turning back to the stove and stirring a pot vigorously—maybe more vigorously than the béchamel I know is inside it requires. "Brit is the best thing that ever happened to you."

There's that pain again, slicing my insides to ribbons, but I shove it down. Ignore it. Like I've had to so many times since I uttered those words in the kitchen of our house months ago.

"Roxie is the best thing that's ever happened to me."

My mom pauses in her stirring, head tilting to the side, eyes like mine piercing into me, making me want to both keep arguing and to avoid the way she sees right through me.

Case in point?

Her tone softening. "That's understood, honey," she murmurs. "But you know that you can have more than one best thing."

I feel that—deep and viscerally and—

The front door swings open, slamming against the wall in the entry with a resounding *thud*. It echoes through the hose, vibrates through the floor, the soles of my shoes like a tiny earthquake.

Kind of like the little girl who's caused it.

I move into the hall.

Rox's feet pound on the floor as she runs toward me. "Dad!"

"Oof, baby girl," I mutter, wrapping my arms around her and scooping her up, holding her against my chest, peppering her cheeks with kisses. "You taste delicious," I tell her, soaking in my cuddles, her giggles, knowing that she's not going to tolerate this for much longer.

"Dad!" she groans, pushing me away. "Gross!"

I steal one more kiss before plunking her down onto her feet. "Okay," I say. "I heard through the grapevine that you did something special today."

"I got two goals in practice!" she says, holding up as many fingers.

My mouth twitches. "That's awesome"—I capture her hand

—"but that's not what I meant." I touch the tip of her finger, painted a bright, glittery red. "These look pretty, honey."

Her whole face lights up. "Tiffany got the same color."

My eyes slide from my daughter's to the woman leaning against the opening to the kitchen. She's beautiful, standing there with her arms folded over her chest, ankles crossed, mouth curved into a small smile.

"Tiffany and you have good taste," I murmur.

"Can I see, baby doll?"

Roxie freezes, surprise and delight on her face, clearly not having put together that the delicious smell in the air signaled Grandma's presence. Then she unsticks just as quickly. "Grandma!" she shouts, sprinting toward my mom.

Cuddles are exchanged.

Nails are admired.

Days are caught up on.

And then we all sit down to eat some lasagna.

And I do it, trying to ignore that my life feels like it's got a giant hole in it.

A hole that's, perhaps, the size of a five-foot-ten, slender blonde with a killer glove hand.

Four

BRIT

He's bringing the puck across the blue line, skating toward me with a speed that has me fighting my instincts.

To slow down.

To back up.

To retreat and give him space.

But that's the wrong move.

One hundred percent the wrong move.

That will give the skater—the potential shooter—far too much space to make trouble for me. Better angles to shoot, more room, more time to make a move and score.

So, I fight that initial instinct and push through, charging out beyond the top of the crease—that semi-circle of blue paint in a rapid flash of motion. The move cuts off his angles, gives him less room to shoot, puts him on his heels a little.

Because all that space he thought he had?

It's gone.

I don't watch his hands. Or his face. And I'm only obliquely keeping track of the puck.

I'm locked in on his hips.

Because his hands can fuck around, the stick an extension of them. His shoulders can zig and zag, as he ducks and dodges, attempting to fake me out. But Shakira's right—the hips don't lie. He can't move without them.

And—

That.

Right there.

He leans to the left, but I see the shift in weight before he moves hard to the right.

And I'm ready.

I dig my skate blade into the ice, ready, waiting...

Go!

My side twinges with a sharp slice of pain, protesting against the movement. All the rehab in the world can't make all of it go away, but I push through. I'm used to pain at this point, used to grinding through, ignoring, playing, *living.*

Bruises and broken bones.

Cuts and torn muscles.

Fatigue and lungs feeling like they're going to explode.

And still...finding a way to play hockey.

I cut hard to the side, waiting until he's close, knowing he's committed to the move, making sure if he can transition to a shot —and he damned well can, because these guys are good, *fucking great*, and they can switch between a move, a shot, a pass, and back again in an instant—it won't be a good one.

Because *I'm* good.

I'm fucking *great.*

So, I can hang with him. I can transition. I can handle whatever he throws at me.

Which is a doozy—cutting hard back to the center, making me scramble to mirror his movements. My side is a wildfire of sensation, of protests and anger and pain and frustration.

But I'm here, and I'm living and pushing through and—

I grunt as I dig my skate in, as I wrench myself in the other direction as he cuts sharply back the other way.

Calm.

Calm.

Don't panic. Stay centered. Stay facing the puck. Stay up. Stay ready and—

"Now," I whisper, whipping to the side, jabbing my stick forward, forcing him to move. To shoot.

When *I'm* ready.

And I am.

I watch his weight shift, and I'm moving before the puck's even left his stick, swinging my arm up, glove open, ready, waiting—

Smack!

The puck hits my palm, the sting reverberating up my arm, into my shoulder, but my hand's closing, holding tight to that disc of vulcanized rubber.

No fucking chance of dropping it, of giving this asshole another chance to score.

I hold tight and wait for the whistle.

Which comes—a sharp *trill* that echoes through the rink...

A bare heartbeat before the fucker crashes right into me.

———

I wince as I move into the house, just lifting my foot the six inches to settle it on the top of the step is agony, and it's just as bad climbing the other two in order to make it inside.

But I get there, turning the handle, pushing the door open, moving into the mudroom.

Backpack on the hook, shoes painfully toed off, my side on absolute fire, but I manage to get them off my feet, get them tucked onto the shoe rack, and then I hobble down the hallway.

I'm getting old.

Not even trainer extraordinaire Mandy and all her magical rehabilitation tricks can change that fact.

She can treat my bruises, can bandage a sore joint, can rehab an injury with the best of them.

But...the wear and tear that comes with playing this sport, with these long seasons, the eighty-two games, the four rounds of playoffs, with...getting older and sliding down the leeward slope of my career—

That's not something she can fix.

It's why I retired a few seasons ago, before I was lured back with the promise of just one more.

One more season. One more chance at the Cup. One more year of what I knew before everything changed.

But that season turned into more than one.

And then my chance was almost torn away, that choice almost stolen from me.

And...

I couldn't let it go.

Now, I'm right back here again.

Hurting. Old. Knowing retirement is looming, all those changes bearing down on me anyway.

Only, what do I have for it?

My name on a silver trophy—three times.

My number likely to soon be hanging from the rafters.

My name in the record books.

And...

What do I have to show for it?

I exhale—the pain not just in my body now, but in my soul, my heart—and start moving down the hall. Food. Sleep. Push it down and keep moving forward.

I walk quietly toward the kitchen, the soft glow of the under-cabinet lights I left on shining out, guiding my way.

Because I don't have someone to leave them on for me.

Not any longer.

Sara—one of my good friends and wife of a former teammate,

Mike Stewart (who's a good friend too)—is doing me a solid by putting Rox to bed, staying with her until I get back, but I know I can't continue relying on my friends to take turns watching my kid on my custody days.

I need to hire someone.

I need to take responsibility and deal with this shit already.

I just...I just thought that—

Well, I thought it might be a nightmare...one I could wake from. One I could come back from.

Only...

Time has told me that isn't going to happen.

My eyes sting, but—like usual—I ignore them, ignore the burn, ignore the pain.

Food. Sleep. Roxie. Hockey.

That's all I've got.

I turn, move into the kitchen, and—

The sound that comes out of me is part hurt, part panic, part...hope.

Because Stefan is sitting on that barstool.

The same one he was sitting on when he broke my heart all those months ago.

FIVE

STEFAN

I've sat here hundreds of times before.

Waiting for the door to the garage to open with a soft squeak, to listen to the rustle of fabric as Brit hangs up her backpack, her coat, tucks her shoes onto the rack.

The padding footsteps down the hall.

The woman who owns my heart coming around the corner—

Owned.

She *owned* my heart. It has to be owned because otherwise I can't—

I exhale silently, brace against the presence of her.

She's beautiful, as always. Hair pulled back into a tight ponytail, not a lick of makeup on her face, lean female body wearing a long sleeve tee and sweats. No nonsense.

Fucking gorgeous.

Always.

But I don't focus on the stupidity of that thought, because I'm moving, pushing up from the barstool, crossing over to her.

"You're hurting," I murmur, seeing the truth of that in her chocolate-brown eyes.

Even though she shakes her head, mouth curving into a smile that's so fucking fake, it's not even funny. "I'm fine." She moves past me, every goddamned step a lesson in fighting through pain. "Why are you here?" she asks before I can call her on her bullshit.

"Ben"—the son of one of our good friends, Mike Stewart— "fell during soccer and broke his arm. Sara didn't want to worry you before game time, so she asked if I could cover for a couple of hours."

"Oh." A long pause before she clears her throat. "Well, thanks," she murmurs, pulling open the fridge, surveying the contents like she's not going to grab out a chocolate milk and a container of veggies and hummus like she always does.

The only question is if she's going to have cucumbers, peppers, and carrots, or cucumbers, peppers, and kale.

Curious, I lean to the side as she pops open the top—

And some part of my stomach twists as I see that the variable isn't kale or carrots, or even snap peas, but—

"You hate broccoli," I blurt.

She stills, the lid clenched in her hand, but then she unlocks, moving stiffly to the sink, setting it in the sink with a soft *plink*. She picks up the container, brings it to the island, turns for the fridge.

But I've beaten her to it, opening the door again, pulling out the container of hummus.

"Here," I murmur, handing it over.

Our fingers brush, that little spark of sensation the contact sends through me exactly the same as it was when I first touched her.

And she seems to feel it too, body jerking and then a wince dragging across her face.

"You're hurting," I say again.

At least this time she doesn't deny it. Instead, she just gives a miniscule shrug. "That's the life," she says. "As you well know." Then she brings the hummus to the counter, takes a spoon from the utensil drawer, and slops some over her veggies.

"Brit—"

It feels weird to use her name.

To not call her baby or sweetheart.

And it causes the rest of my words to stopper up in my throat.

"I'm sorry you got called in for kiddo duty on your day off," she whispers.

A bolt of irritation slides through me. "It's not kid duty," I say. "Roxie is my daughter, and if she needs me, I'll always be there for her."

The pain that cuts across her face is so sharp that I freeze, instinctively looking around for a threat, then to her body, searching for evidence that she's been wounded.

Only she's uninjured.

On the outside anyway.

"What?" I ask.

"Nothing," she says, taking the container and her chocolate milk in hand and nodding toward the front door. "I'll walk you out," she says. "I need to eat and go to sleep."

She doesn't wait for me to answer, just starts walking—or hobbling rather—leading me out of my own fucking house.

Walking across tile I helped select, pictures I hung on the wall, a table we built together on a bleary-eyed evening when Roxie was sick and not sleeping.

"What?" I say again, the memories beating at me.

The chip in the corner of the opening when Blane—another teammate—and I were moving furniture in right after we bought the place. One I promised myself I would fix.

And clearly didn't.

A row of hooks, plenty big for all of the Gold contingent to hang jackets and purses and diaper bags when they come over for our Christmas Pie Extravaganza.

Something Brit organizes and people love.

Something I won't go to this year because—

I try to shove the memories down, but they don't stop lashing out at me.

Birthday parties and a couch stained red with frosting from a dropped cupcake.

Brit smiling at the crying kiddo, telling them not to worry, that it would come out.

Spoiler alert—it didn't.

Roxie roller-skating through the halls, Brit holding her up, not caring about the finish on the floor, about the scratches that were the inevitable conclusion. Not when it meant that Rox was having the time of her life while making a core memory.

"What went through your head in the kitchen?" I ask—*too* loudly because she jumps. But I'm trying to drown out the sounds of those memories.

I have to.

I *have* to.

She straightens her shoulders, long blond ponytail swinging behind her, and reaches for the lock. But I move without thinking, snagging her arm, wrapping my fingers around her wrist, stopping her from turning it.

"What?" I say again, stepping close.

Too close.

So fucking close that our bodies drift together, meld in a familiar decades-old pattern that we've assumed a hundred, a thousand times before. Her hips shift to cradle mine, my thigh slides between hers, our chests brush, our lips part, breaths mingling.

So easy to close the distance. To taste her.

But...

That won't solve anything.

That'll—

Fuck things up even more.

"Back up," she says, eyes clearing of the softness, of the sparks of desire our bodies have never had an issue creating.

"No." A beat, ignoring the outrage dancing across her expression. "Tell me what you thought back there."

"Nothing."

I drop a hand next to her head, move until we're plastered together, toes to chest. "*Brit.*"

My cock twitches.

My balls ache.

Wrong. This is wrong.

But it's too late.

Our closeness or her name on my tongue...one of those seems to shake things loose. "You used to say that to me," she says softly. "Used to be that *for* me."

I frown, trying to process her words.

But then she continues speaking.

And the pieces come together with razor-sharp clarity.

"You promised if I needed you," she whispers. "You promised you would be here for me. Always. And—" She presses her lips together, head jerking to the side.

But not before I see the tears glimmering in her eyes.

Not before I begin to hate myself.

No.

That's already been firmly in place for a while now.

"I wasn't," I tell her.

Her shoulders hitch up, and she shoves me away, starts back down the hall. "No, Stefan"—not *honey*, not *baby*, not *sweetheart*—"you weren't." She sighs. "But—as you pointed out rather effectively when you asked for the divorce—neither was I."

I move without thinking.

But it has unintended consequences, crowding her so quickly that I know the past rears up and smacks her hard across the face—forces her to remember another time when a man, when *men*, crowded her and hurt her and—

She stumbles even though I don't get close enough to touch her, tripping backward over her feet and going down hard.

I reach out a hand, try to catch her.

But I'm living with the blow of scaring her, of hurting her like those assholes from her past did, and I don't react in time.

She hits the floor with a pained grunt.

One that's much more intense than a simple fall to the floor.
One that's filled with agony.
And...
I stop thinking.

Six

P ain tears through my side, ripples through my torso.

I freeze, every muscle going tight, bracing as the avalanche of hurt tumbles over me. Waiting as it pummels me over and over and *over*. Until, finally, the pain begins to subside.

My eyes are clenched tight, so I don't see Stefan moving closer.

But I feel him.

Feel the brush of his hand on my cheek, the roughened skin of his palm, his calloused fingertips running so fucking gently over my skin. "Breathe, sweetheart," his soft voice rumbles, "just breathe through the worst of it."

My physical body hurts—from the fall, from my past injuries.

But those words hurt more.

Or maybe the tone.

Or maybe the touch—his hand shifting, cupping my jaw, sliding down along the outside of my throat, and then his weight shifts and I'm gasping as I'm suddenly in his arms, cradled against his chest.

Like I mean something.

Like I mean something to *him*.

"N-no," I stutter, shoving at the arm banded around my middle, kicking my legs against his hold on my knees.

For all the good it does me.

Because his arms just tighten and then he's straightening, moving toward the stairs, carrying me up them.

"What are you—?"

"Hush," he whispers, and—God—this hurts so much that I can't continue talking, can't form that protest on my tongue, my lips, can't keep fighting him as he carries me into the bedroom and sets me on the bed with a softly ordered, "Stay."

My eyes are burning. My jaw pulses with pain as I clench it tightly.

And then he's gone.

And...I don't stay.

I can't.

I push up from the mattress, from the bed I slept beside this man in for more than a decade, and I move painfully into the closet, snatching clothes at random—sweats, tank, socks, and a hoodie. Then I'm in the bathroom, the door closing behind me with a soft *click*. I flick the lock, move to the counter, and drop the clothes on top.

Unfortunately, doing so means that I catch a glimpse of myself in the reflection of the mirror.

And I don't recognize the woman staring back at me.

Older. With far more gray hairs and wrinkles than a decade before. And with...shadows in my eyes again.

Shadows I'd excised once.

Shadows...that are back.

"Enough," I whisper, moving carefully as I unzip my Gold branded sweatshirt, drop it to the floor, as I wrestle my Gold branded T-shirt and bra over my head, ignoring the pain radiating up my spine, through my side and arms and legs.

My entire body is one raw nerve.

But I ignore that too as I drop my pants to the ground, toe off my socks, my underwear.

And swap them for fresh pairs. My extra comfy underwear. My fuzzy socks. Sweats that fit loose and feel like silk. A tank that's thin and soft and perfect beneath my San Francisco tie-dye hoodie that Roxie picked out for me the last time we were down at the tourist trap that is Pier 39.

Noise and crowds and freshly baked sourdough. Sea lions protesting.

Managing the rides and getting her snacks and fans coming up for autographs and...

Doing it alone.

Because I'm a single parent.

My heart squeezes, the ache intensifying, but I push it down and finish getting ready for bed. Teeth brushed and flossed—can't risk my sponsored and billboard-adorning smile. Face moisturized —because that's just a good habit to have. Hair combed and braided—so it doesn't get in my mouth and eyes and wrap around my throat, threatening to asphyxiate me.

Then I have no choice but to go back out the bathroom door.

And I already know that Stefan's going to be standing there, exactly *there*—leaning against the open doorway.

But I don't see him—or he's not the *first* thing I see.

Instead, my gaze hits on my nightstand, on the container of veggies and hummus, on the chocolate milk sitting next to it.

My heart convulses.

But I lock it down, turn to face the man who was my heart... and then shattered it.

He's holding a container of bruise cream. It's a special concoction made by the team's head trainer—Mandy—and it works like nothing else.

Another squeeze in my chest, so fierce that pain ripples through my torso again.

"You need to go," I say, moving toward him, snatching the container of cream from his hand and setting it on the built-in shelves that surround the TV, that are filled with all my favorite smutty books that Mandy, Sara, and I—and anyone else who wants to join in on—read during our monthly book club. Shelves this man insisted I have.

More pain in my chest.

More things to just shove down, *down*.

"Brit."

Goddamn it.

I clench my teeth, shove by him, my body protesting, but my heart protesting more. I can't look into those blue eyes any longer.

"*Brit*," he says again. "Where are you going?"

Anywhere you aren't.

Thankfully, I manage to not say that out loud as I walk quickly down the hall, as I quietly open the door and peek in on my baby girl. Rox is sprawled out on her back, arms and legs akimbo, blanket kicked off as always.

I pick my way through the detritus of stuffed animals and dirty clothes, hair ties and Nerf guns to get to her bedside, to tug it up and over her little body, to tuck it snuggly around her.

Safe. Protected.

Sleeping soundly.

All I've ever wanted for my little girl.

I reset her nightlight so it won't turn off until the sun comes up, the darkness in her room no longer an invisible threat, and then pick my way back to the door, closing it silently behind me.

Stefan, unfortunately, hasn't disappeared.

"Look," I say, softly, "I'm tired, and I'm sure you're tired too."

He just spins on his heel, walks away from me, and the sight is so much like that night, the night he left, the night he asked for a divorce that I'm frozen there for a moment, a giant ball of hurt.

Then I realize he's walking into my bedroom, and not down the stairs, not out the front door, and I snap out of it.

"What the fuck are you doing?" I snap as I hobble after him.

He ignores me, nods to the bed. "Lie down."

A flicker of heat between my thighs before I regain control of myself. "Go home."

Which isn't fucking *here*.

He just continues to ignore me, moving to the shelves, picking up the jar of bruise cream, shoulders stiffening as his eyes drag across a book sitting sideways on top of the other books.

And there my heart goes again.

Because...

We had fun acting that book out.

He moves to the bed, nods his head sharply. "Lie down."

"You need to go home."

He unscrews the lid, tosses it on the nightstand. "Brit, just lie the *fuck* down."

I dig my toes into the carpet, grind my teeth together. "Stefan—"

His eyes flash, and I see it on his face.

He's not going to give.

And I'm tired. I'm exhausted. I'm ready to pass out and sleep until this is all a faint memory.

Maybe that's why I do what I do next.

I exhale quietly and move to the bed. I ignore the spicy scent of him as I climb onto the mattress, arms folded and face shoved into the pillow, bracing, waiting, wishing for it to both happen and not, all at the same time.

And then it does.

Fingers go to the hem of my hoodie, tug it up, exposing my naked skin to the cool evening air. "You never used to wear so many clothes to bed," he murmurs.

I freeze then I lift my chin, twisting my neck so I can glance over at him. "I get cold now."

His blue eyes cool, sending a shiver through me, but I just ignore it, ignore him because my eyes are catching on the faint pink scar on my side, mostly hidden by Roxie's name...which is mostly hidden *today* courtesy of the giant bruise blooming on my side.

Then I settle my forehead back onto the pillow, grit my teeth, and promise myself that I just have to endure this one thing.

Then I can sleep.

I hear the *glop* of him scooping from the container of bruise cream, the slick sounds that remind me of other slick sounds—

Enough.

I jump as cold fingertips hit my skin, sending a bolt of pain through me, but then his fingers are moving, smoothing over my side, lightly rubbing the cream in, spreading it all along my flesh.

Goose bumps and more heat between my legs.

But I ignore it.

Ignore him.

And pretty soon fatigue is sinking its claws into me, pulling me down, down, *down* into oblivion, until when Stefan finally speaks—his voice almost hushed—I barely hear it.

"This is pretty bad," he murmurs. "Are you going to take a couple of days off?"

My lids flash open.

I turn my head, eyes catching his.

"No."

I'd intended for it to come out of *my* mouth, but he's beaten me to it.

"No," he says again, voice hardening. "Of course you're not going to take any time off. Of course you're not going to stop—"

He jerks his hand away, and the loss of his touch...well, goddamn, it's just another punch to the ribs. And then he's tugging my tank top down, my hoodie, pushing up to his feet.

The jar of cream hits the nightstand, sending the lid toppling to the floor, my vegetables rattling softly in their glass container.

A sigh. "Broccoli," I swear he whispers. "Jesus Christ."

But before I get a chance to respond to that, get the chance to make that make sense, he's turning for the door.

Before I get a chance to respond...

He's gone.

And I'm still exhausted and hurting and more than ready for sleep.

But...

That blissful oblivion doesn't come.

SEVEN

STEFAN

I thumb a text to Tiffany as I walk into Roxie's school, running a few minutes behind and all the more annoyed for it.

I hate being late, and especially hate being late for important shit.

And Roxie's parent-teacher conference is *really* important shit.

I wave at the receptionists—getting a scowl from the grumpy one and a smile from the other one (who partook in my baked-goods-from-Molly's bribe at the beginning of the school year)—and hurry across the blacktop to Roxie's classroom.

But what I see outside the closed metal door has rage splintering through me.

It shouldn't.

But it does.

Brit is standing next to a man who's objectively good-looking—something I want to gouge my eyes out for noticing. But I *do* notice. That he's tall and built and in good shape. That he's looking at my wife with far too much concentration, far too much focus, far too much...*need*. My hands ball into fists, and I take a step toward them, intending on knocking the motherfucker through that cinderblock wall they're leaning back against.

I stop.

I freeze.

I exhale.

Ex-wife.

Ex-*fucking* wife.

"Ex-wife," I whisper aloud. And that's finally enough to snap me out of it, to make me remember, to see reason. I push out a breath through my nose, tuck away the anger I don't have any right to feel, and move over to them.

"...and I was thinking," the man says. "If you're not doing anything tomorrow, maybe we could go grab a drink—"

Rage flares anew, blasting through the shield I'd erected around my emotions, around that possessiveness, around the past.

Was this motherfucker asking *my* woman out on a fucking *date*?

I'm going to kill him.

I'm going to slice him into a thousand pieces.

Brit's shoulders hitch up, clearly recognizing the same shit I do, and uncomfortable with it.

Her teeth press into her bottom lip, eyes darting to the side, away from the asshole in front of her.

"—or," the dumb fuck says, "we can go for a coffee—"

"She doesn't like coffee," I snap, making them both turn around.

"I—uh—I—" The dipshit stammers, off-kilter either because the ex-husband of the woman he's trying to hit on is two feet away, or because his pickup of my ex-wife isn't going as planned.

Brit's gaze comes to mine, eyes narrowing, brows pulling into a deep frown. "What are you doing?" she mouths.

I flick *my* brows up, challenging her. "Saving you from this dipshit," I mouth back.

She comes closer, rises on tiptoe, mouth coming very close to my ear that has my balls, my dick remembering that mouth, those lips, that tongue other places—*better* fucking places. "I don't need saving from this dipshit," she hisses. "And I don't need you to save *me*." Then she drops back onto her heels, turns to face Dipshit McGee and says, "How about a run instead?"

I inhale sharply.

Because that's *our* thing.

Was our thing.

Dipshit's eyes go wide, but he's already nodding like one of those bobbleheads they give away at the Gold Mine, flopping his skull around like an idiot. "A run sounds great."

I snort, drawing both of their focus.

Brit is glaring.

Dipshit is...dipshitting—and more importantly, he doesn't realize what he just agreed to. Brit is a fucking professional athlete, and yeah, she's nearing forty, but she's also one of the fastest runners I've ever met.

This fucker has no idea what kind of torture he's just signed up for.

"Ignore him," Brit says, pulling out her cell. "Why don't you give me your number and we can arrange a time?"

"Kind of like we've arranged a time for a parent-teacher conference?" I ask archly—and also like an asshole.

Because...I'm an asshole.

"Yes," she says, eyes shooting sparks at me. "One you were late for, so I told Ms. Carlson to feel free to step out and make the phone call she needed to make?"

Yup. *Asshole.*

"Trey was just finishing up with his timeslot when I came." She flashes me a smile that's all teeth and absolutely no amusement. "Because he was *on time*."

Jibe. Snap. Dig.

I fucking hate this part of breaking up.

So why did you ask for a divorce, asshole?

Because—

"Oh, great," a female voice says from behind me, "you're both here." I turn to see Ms. Carlson coming toward us, tucking her cell into the pocket of her flowing black slacks. "Sorry to keep you waiting."

"Don't apologize," Brit tells her. "Stefan just got here, and we were all catching up. Is your son okay?"

Ms. Carlson smiles exasperatedly. "He's fine. Just couldn't find his lacrosse stick."

Brit laughs. "Sounds about right."

Ms. Carlson unlocks the door, holds it open. "Should we go in?"

"Yeah," I mutter, starting forward. "We should go in. Right, Brit?"

Her shoulders stiffen and she opens her mouth—

Trey—God, what a dipshit name—snags her cell from her hand and jabs at the screen, presumably programming his number in.

And, swear to fuck, I didn't think the little dick had it in him. He hands it back, murmurs, "I'll look for your text."

Jesus.

I don't know whether to congratulate him on a job well done, or to punch the fucker over and over again until he ceases breathing.

The second one.

Definitely the second one.

But I don't get the chance because then Brit is smiling at Trey —and it's a real fucking smile, and I hate it, and—

"Talk to you soon," she murmurs to him.

Then she walks into the classroom, eyes deliberately not coming to mine.

And I have to follow behind her.

Have to act like everything is okay, like everything is fine.

Like everything is exactly how it should be.

Just...my wife arranging a date with another man.

Ex-wife.

No big deal.

Eight

BRIT

I groan and flop back on my bed. "What the hell am I doing, Sara?"

My friend—one of my closest and longest and bestest (yes, I'm actually using the word bestest like a tween girl...probably because I feel like one, like a young girl getting ready to go on her first date)—stares over at me from the disorganized chaos of my closet. "You're moving on, honey," she says gently. "And"—a pause long enough that my heart begins to pound, begins to throw itself against my rib cage, "it's about time."

I clench my teeth together.

I barely resist shaking my head.

But I do...and then I manage to focus on more important things like, "Why are you so worried about what I'm going to wear?" I ask, shoving myself upright. "We're literally going for a run and then the juice bar. Joggers and a tee are a requisite for that."

Sara pauses, tiny former figure skating body outlined in the light of my closet.

Then she shakes her head and sighs.

Then she tosses some clothes in my direction. "At least wear that."

I scowl at the tight black leggings, the strappy sports bra, the flowy tank to wear over the top. "Sara," I warn.

"This is your first date in—"

"Don't," I whisper.

She sighs, walks across the room in that graceful way of hers, then flops onto the bed next to me. "I know it hurts, honey."

I turn my head away, slam my eyes closed.

"I don't know why he did it. I don't get it. Neither do Mike or Blane or any of the guys." Another sigh. "But he *did* do it, babe."

"I didn't help," I whisper, all of those insecurities welling up. "I-I—I'm not an easy woman to love—"

The bed rocking is the only warning I get before Sara's fingers are wrapping around my chin, sending my eyes shooting open. She yanks my face toward her, and she's wearing a fierce expression I so rarely see now that all the rough and jagged edges of her have been soothed by years and years with her husband, Mike.

"You are *so* easy to love," she says, fingers tightening when I start to look away again. "You are so fucking easy to love, honey."

My vision is blurry and I'm barely hanging on.

Luckily, my bestie recognizes that.

She releases me, pops up off the bed. "So stop with that shit. Wear the clothes that will show off that gorgeous body of yours. Enjoy your run and your juice and a cute boy—or man. Let that be the first step to moving forward, babe. To allowing yourself to be happy."

I inhale, holding the air in my lungs long enough for them to protest. Only then do I exhale, murmuring, "I *am* happy."

My friend takes my hand, squeezes it lightly. "Well then, you're allowed to be happier, okay?"

"I am—"

Her cell rings, and she sighs, shaking her head. "That's school's ringtone. I need to get it."

I start to sit up. "Of course you do," I tell her.

Another squeeze of her hand. "You've got this, Banana." And then she's unlacing our fingers, reaching into her pocket, pulling out her cell. "Hello?"

Then she goes stiff, drops her chin to her chest. "Again?" she asks tone full of resignation. "Yeah," she says a moment later. "I'll be right there." She hangs up, sighs, and shakes her head as she shoves her phone back into her pocket. "My kid is a bull in a china shop."

"What happened?"

"He was playing Wall Ball"—this being a new playground game that all the kids at our local elementary school are obsessed with—"and he somehow ran himself into the wall instead of the ball."

My lips twitch, something I try to push down, but something that Sara catches anyway.

Because she nudges my shoulder. "I know what you're thinking—"

"That how can two people as athletically talented as you and Mike—a gold medalist figure skater, a professional hockey player—somehow produce a kid as uncoordinated as your youngest?"

She wrinkles her nose. "Yes." A sigh. "That." She wraps her arms around me. "You've got this, honey. Just keep hanging in there until it feels less like hanging and more like soaring."

"So says the figure skater who can leap and twirl through the sky."

"Okay," she teases. "Keep hanging in there until every puck hits the dead center of your glove."

"That's better." I nod toward the door. "Go," I say. "I'm fine. I promise."

She exhales, head dropping back. "Please no concussions," she prays. "I am not prepared to spend another day in the ER."

"Keep me posted and let me know if you need me to grab the other kiddos."

Sara lifts her head, expression soft, and then reaches over and hugs me tight. "You are beautiful. You are worthy. You are loveable."

Those words hit like a barrage of pucks colliding on my pads during practice. *Bam! Bam! Bam!* And as I'm absorbing the impact, she's dropping her arms, stepping back.

"Bye, honey. I'll text you." She moves to the door, hesitates on the threshold. "Brit?"

I'm reaching for the leggings, but pause, my fingers wrapped in the stretchy black fabric. I look back up at my friend. "Be happy, honey."

Another puck, this time to the stomach, stinging through my chest protector. "Thanks, Sara."

Then she's gone.

And then I'm pulling on those leggings, that pretty strappy bra, the flowy tank.

I push my feet into my sneakers, pull my hair up into a pony-tail, grab a hoodie because it's inevitably going to start off cold.

Mascara and a tinted moisturizer. A bit of blush and some lip gloss.

"And that's as good as it's going to get," I whisper.

I exhale.

And then I walk out of my house.

And...

I go for a run.

NINE

STEFAN

"I like them a lot, baby girl," my mom says, admiring the newest manicure that Rox is sporting—blue sparkles and one white nail with a glittery crystal design glued onto it.

Heaven forbid one of those falls off on the ice during practice or a game and ruins someone's skate blade.

Disaster.

Except, she's playing in-house hockey at the local rink.

For *fun.*

Everyone's edges are already either over or under sharpened. There aren't any blades to ruin.

No million-dollar contracts. No twenty-thousand seat arena jam-packed with screaming fans. No Cup to heft.

Just Rox and her buddies.

And she loves glitter and sparkles and rhinestones.

So, she gets glitter and sparkles and rhinestones.

"Whatcha think, Dad?" she asks, flashing her hand in my direction, sending Tiffany smiling behind her.

"Hmm," I say, carefully inspecting them even though she's

shown me the design at least five times since she and Tiff got home. "I think they're beautiful nails for a beautiful girl."

She smiles widely, presses her lips to my cheek in a sloppy kiss, and I scoop her close, pretending to eat her ear, making her laugh, those giggles the best sound on the planet. But—all too soon she's squirming and I have to put her down, have let her run across the room to my dad. "Come on, Grandpa," she says, taking his hand and drawing him forward. "I'm ready for our sleepover!"

Then she's tugging him—Pierre Barie, owner of the Gold and several multibillion-dollar companies—toward the front door like she's an excited puppy on her first walk. Tiffany follows with Roxie's overnight bag, stuffed to the brim with Squishmallows of all plush, cuddly sizes. I watch as my mom sends another disapproving look my direction before moving to the rack just inside the door, pulls off her jacket, and shrugs it on. And then she slips her purse from the hook, hangs it over her shoulder.

And all the while, I can feel her condemnation.

It's not a new emotion.

She's filled the room with it—anytime it's the two of us—ever since I asked for the divorce.

It's there—a palpable force that runs over my skin like sandpaper. And I know the only thing that'll make it go away is to do something that I can't.

Go back.

Fix it.

Make it so it never happened.

I can't—fucking *can't*.

Something she knows—or at least understands somewhat—because she just crosses the room, presses a kiss to my cheek. "We'll meet you for breakfast tomorrow."

"Let me know if she or you need anything," I tell her, hugging her carefully, knowing that I'm lucky to have her here, that she battled to stay on the earth for us.

"I will, baby," she murmurs, disapproval finally softening as her eyes come to mine, her brows flicking up. "You'll do the same?"

"I'll be fine."

She huffs out a breath, shakes her head. "Sure you will," she mutters, but she walks out the front door when I hold it open for her, heads down the path.

My dad is at his car, watching as Roxie buckles herself into her booster seat.

A booster seat in Pierre Barie's car.

Will wonders ever fucking cease?

That, at least, sends a bolt of amusement through me, the first in far too fucking long.

Amusement that lasts precisely one more heartbeat.

Because then I hear Roxie announce—in response to my dad's inquiry about what Brit is up to tonight, "My mom says she's going on another run with her new running friend."

I freeze, a knife jabbing into my insides.

My mom's head whips in my direction, brows lifted almost to her hairline.

Tiff finishes stowing Rox's bag in the trunk and slams it closed, her expression unreadable.

"New running friend?" my dad asks, his tone careful, but his eyes icy as fuck as they flick to mine.

"Yup," Rox tells him, popping the p at the end. "They both like to run on the trails by school. They've gone three"—she holds up three fingers—"times and today they're going to try to get to the top of Redwood Rock."

"Wow," my dad says, frosty eyes clearing before he looks back to Roxie. "That's a long way."

"I know," she says, sitting back and swinging her legs as my dad checks her seat belt. "But my mom is super-*duper* fast, so she'll make it."

Another dagger in my gut—that confidence, that pride, that faith in her mom.

"Don't you think, Dad?" she calls.

I grind my back teeth together. "Oh," I force out, knowing my throat sounds like it's gone six rounds with gargling gravel, "she'll definitely make it."

My dad's lips press flat at my answer, but I watch him deliberately table the reaction, know that we've come a long way in our relationship since he showed back up in my life as an adult.

But I also know that while his disapproval over my ending things with Brit is as palpable as my mother's, he hasn't said one word about it.

Because that's not his place.

Because he's not my mom.

"Can we get ice cream on the way home, Grandpa?" Rox asks.

I open my mouth as I walk toward them. "It's dinner time—"

"Sure, we can, pumpkin," he says, ruffling Roxie's hair.

And completely ignoring me.

Right. Message received and understood.

He's not commenting on my life decisions. But also, he's not engaging with me when it's something he doesn't want to engage with.

Like me divorcing his star player.

Like me telling his granddaughter she should wait for ice cream until after dinner.

My mom sighs, presses her lips to my cheek. "See you in the morning for breakfast."

My dad nods, drops his hand to my shoulder, squeezes lightly. "We'll have your favorites." He grins. "Or maybe we'll just go to Molly's so we can all have our favorites."

"Molly's!" Rox exclaims with a woot.

He's a hard-ass who doesn't approve of every decision I've made. But he's a hard-ass who loves me, my mom, and my kid.

I could do worse.

I nod, clasp my hand around his. "Thanks, Dad."

A jerk of his chin, and then he's pulling back, getting into the driver's seat. I wave goodbye to Roxie, to my mom, to my dad. Then hold back a sigh and I turn toward Tiff.

She smiles as she moves toward me, not stopping until her scent is in my nose, all flowers and vanilla, all soft and feminine and *not* Brit. "So," she says, her lips curving, her eyes coming to mine, "what's up next, hotshot?"

TEN

BRIT

My lungs are burning and sweat is dripping down my back.

It's not even hot, the cool ocean breeze having drifted inward, weaving its way in through the trees, cooling my heated skin.

But it's not enough to beat the exertion of the trail, especially at the pace we're taking it.

Trey is a good running partner. He's not as fast as me, nor in as good of shape—but then again, he's not a professional athlete. Still, he's dogged, determined to make it to the top of the trail even though I know he's got to be feeling it intensely, has to be even more tired than I am.

"We're almost there," I manage to get out...and make it sound as though it's vaguely encouraging (and not like I'm ready to throw myself off the steep decline to the left, if only to put myself out of the misery of this near vertical trail).

"Yup," he puffs out, distance between us increasing.

But if I stop to wait for him, I'll stop altogether.

And...we're almost there.

Really.

I turn the corner—

And I'm there.

My feet slide to a stop, and I can't help but stop this time.

Because the sight in front of me is awe-inspiring. Rolling hills dotted with large old-growth oak trees. I turn—chest still heaving, sweat still running down my back, between my breasts—and I see that view is surrounding me on all sides, a full three-hundred-sixty-degree panorama of nature. Not a house or power line in sight. No roads are visible—except if I maybe squint and study the far edges of my vision, I can see the narrow track that leads into this preserve.

A foot scrapes behind me, and—lungs beginning to recover— I rotate back to see Trey stagger around the corner.

"Sweet Jesus," he puffs, moving toward me. "That was hell—" A long breath before he turns out toward the view and exhales again, clearly trying to slow his heart rate. "And totally fucking worth it." He swipes his arm over his forehead. "Wow."

"Yeah," I say, taking pity on my quads and sinking down onto the rock that gives the Redwood Rock trail its name.

Trey sinks down next to me, groaning as he stretches his legs out in front of him. "Brutal but beautiful." He slants a look at me. "Kind of like you when you stone those motherfuckers on a breakaway."

I grin. "First time I've ever considered being called brutal a compliment."

He winks and there's a resounding flicker in my stomach. The possibility of something. That something might be here. That something might grow. It feels...bittersweet, but I'm choosing to focus on the *sweet*.

Because I have to.

Because if I don't...

I just can't keep focusing on the *bitter*.

We sit there in silence until we've both recovered from the climb enough to start talking about other things—his daughter and his divorce, Stefan and I trying to find our way to something neutral, the team, his job as a corporate accountant, what my travel schedule looks like over the next few weeks.

And then a leaf flutters out of the tree above us, toppling through the air this way and that until...

It lands in my hair.

I laugh softly, reach up to snag it.

But Trey beats me to it. "Here," he murmurs, tugging it free.

I still, suddenly aware of how near he is...and how it makes me feel.

Right and wrong.

Strange and not.

He smooths his hand over my hair, straightening the—no doubt—crazy tendrils, and...I can't help it.

I remember another man, another time when the person I was interested in didn't care that I was sweaty, that my hair was a mess, and—

His lips come closer.

And...I'm stuck in my memories, in this moment of split reality—Stefan stepping close, his hands in my hair; Trey turning as he shifts beside me, his palm cupping my jaw. The arena in the background, the sounds of my teammates in my ears. The quiet of the late afternoon, wind swooshing through the trees. Cool rink air clinging to my cheeks. Fading sunshine gilding my skin.

Right and wrong.

Strange and not.

Stefan. Trey.

Trey. Stefan.

Soft lips touch mine—

Right and wrong.

No.

Wrong.

It's *wrong.*

"No," I whisper, breaking the kiss, pushing lightly at Trey's—yes, it's *Trey's*—chest. Not Stefan's. Not—

"You taste so good," Trey groans, hand tightening in my hair, body coming closer, rolling over mine, pressing me into the rock face.

"*No,*" I say again, my gut churning, bile rising up to burn the back of my throat. I push at his chest more intently, another time of being restrained, of not being able to move, of a man deciding what he's doing with my body pushes into my mind and I struggle to shove it out enough to focus on the present, on this moment. "Stop. This isn't what I want, Trey—"

"*Fuck,*" he rasps. "The way you say my name." He groans again, louder this time, his hand tightening in my hair, more of his weight coming over me...pressing right into my side.

Pain shoots up my torso, and I cry out.

Which seems to make Trey even more earnest—as though he doesn't understand the difference between pain and excitement...

Or maybe that he doesn't care.

More bile. More churning. More pain.

"Stop," I say, ripping my mouth from his when his lips seek mine out a second time. "Trey, *stop—*"

"You want it, baby," he croons, sliding his leg between mine, knee coming up.

Fucking. *Men.*

But before I can react to that—and use some of the self-defense skills Mia (a kickass karate teacher who's married to a teammate and also teaches women how to protect themselves) taught me—I hear a growl.

A fraction of a second later, the weight on top of me disappears.

I blink, shove my elbows beneath me, and freeze. "What the—?"

Only, I don't finish the question.

Because I'm too busy gaping at the sight in front of me.

Stefan is standing there, all of five feet away from me, wearing jeans and a tee, a sweatshirt tied around his waist, and...

He's gripping the front of Trey's shirt, looking a heartbeat away from planting his fist into Trey's face.

"You don't fucking touch her," Stefan growls, shaking Trey like a rag doll. "You. Don't. Fucking. *Touch*. Her."

"Stefan—"

"Not now," he grits out. "Not fucking *ever*. But definitely not after she says *no.*"

And with that, he shoves Trey away, looks over at me, eyes sparking with fire. "Let's go," he snaps. But his hand is gentle when he bends and wraps it around my arm, when he coaxes me up to my feet.

"Brit—"

I freeze at the sound of Trey's voice, turning slowly.

He looks like a confused puppy, unsure of why he just got scolded for chewing a shoe.

"I told you no," I say, watching as his expression changes...

As a thread of something I don't like—irritation, defiance, frustration—weaves across his face. "You liked it."

"No," I tell him. "I didn't like it and I didn't want it." Stefan's fingers tighten on my arm and I pull my gaze away from Trey's, look up at my ex-husband.

"Let's go," he says, and it's softer now.

Because I know he gets what I'm feeling, understands exactly which memories are clambering at the edges of my mind, making my hands shake and my legs feel weak.

So...I go with him.

I let him hold my arm as he guides me down the path, away from that big, warm rock and the late afternoon sunshine, down into the thick cover of the oak trees, their leaves rustling the only sound other than the crunch of our shoes on the rocky trail.

I let him stay close until the parking lot comes into sight, the dark brown fence posts surrounding it visible above the tall, dry grass. There's a large cattle gate across the main entrance and I pull out of Stefan's hold, move to the gate and push it open.

He hesitates for a moment, jaw tight, body still, then he

shakes his head slightly and follows me through. "Where's your car parked?" he asks as we start across the gravel.

"I—"

Here I do something stupid.

I falter.

I freeze.

I don't have a lie at the ready.

And he takes one look at my face and knows it. "You rode with him."

My lungs expand, shoulders lifting and falling on a breath. "First time."

Silence except for the wind.

Then he shakes his head, starts moving toward his car. He *bleeps* the locks, pulls open the door. "I'll drive you home."

Eleven

Stefan

I'm a fucking idiot.

I shouldn't be here.

I shouldn't have intervened between her and that asshole —not for the reasons I had, anyway.

It would be convenient for me to pretend that I did because she was a woman in trouble, that I was the kind of man who would have intervened even if it *wasn't* Brit.

But that would be a fucking lie.

Because, yes, I was a man who wouldn't stand by and let someone be abused or hurt or assaulted, not when there was something I could do about it.

But that wasn't why I'd intervened—or not the *only* reason.

I'd started moving toward Brit and that douchebag the moment I came around the corner and saw them pressed together —my mind shutting down, rage slicing through me...

Possessiveness and anger and...

Well, I'd been ready to tear that fucker to shreds even *before* I heard her tell him no.

And *after* that point?

Murder was the *first* thing on my mind.

Still. Fucking stupid.

Brit is my ex. The papers are filed. The news is all over the media. It's all but official.

But...

Seeing another man touch her—

Christ.

Grinding my teeth together, I clench the steering wheel so fiercely that it creaks in protest.

I need to get the fuck out of this car. I need to get the fuck away from her.

A feeling Brit notices—because of course she does.

Intuitive, smart, and with a heart that's as gold as the glittering metallic nugget that's the team's mascot, Goldie.

"You can drop me off anywhere," she says. "I'll get a Lyft home."

And she means it.

Not passive aggressively. Not with bitterness.

She cares about people and their comfort and what makes them happy—she somehow still even cares about me, her asshole ex.

Some might think that makes her stupid. But she's not. She's got that heart. And they don't get it, don't get her. It's the same as people who think she's too bright, too loud, too outspoken, that she takes up too much space in an area that should belong solely to men.

Dumbasses. Because Brit deserves that space, has more than earned the right to burn brightly and take up room in a male-dominated sport, to just...be herself.

Her kind, thoughtful self.

Case in point? Her pulling out her cell before I get the chance to answer, tapping at the screen, pulling up the rideshare app.

Her kind, thoughtful, *stubborn as shit* (because professional hockey players can't make it to the NHL without being stubborn) self. Which means, I know that even if I reassure her that

I'm not pissed about taking her home (a lie because I am, just not for the reasons she would expect), she will still call for the Lyft and tuck and roll her ass out of my car.

I reach over, snag her phone from her hand, and shove it into the plastic pocket built into the door.

Then hit the locks—even though they automatically engage —just for good measure.

"What the hell, Stefan—?"

"I said I'd drive you home," I mutter, tightening my grip on the steering wheel even further, ignoring the protesting plastic and leather. "I'll get you home."

Silence.

That is unusual.

And it draws my focus, tears my gaze from the road.

Her hands are in her lap, fingers weaved together so tightly that her knuckles are standing out sharply in relief.

But she doesn't comment on my statements, on me taking her phone.

Instead, her shoulders are hitched up, her jaw is tight, and her stare is firmly pointed out the windshield.

"Brit."

She doesn't look at me, doesn't acknowledge me.

I want her to.

I want to demand she does so.

Because I'm a fucking asshole.

"I'll get you home," I say again, and it's less to her and more to myself, more to focus my dumbass brain. To focus on the task at hand.

And on the road.

Not on my ex-wife. Not on the fact that she was on a date that almost ended badly.

Because of decisions *I* made.

Because—

"I know," she says, gaze still on the windshield.

I don't like her tone, hate the dead sound in those two words.

And I don't like that I'm part of what has caused that—extinguishing the bright, making her go quiet and—

A horn bleeps behind me, jerks my eyes away from her profile.

I glance up, see the light's green.

Fuck.

I hit the gas, pull forward, driving along the winding highway until I'm navigating onto the bigger one, grinding my teeth through the usual stop and go that comes with more cars on the road. Then I'm taking the off-ramp and steering us through the familiar quiet, tree-lined neighborhood that leads to my house—

No.

To *Brit's* house.

Where I park in the driveway instead of the garage.

And ignore the fact that it feels wrong.

"Thanks," she says, popping the door the moment I've drawn to a halt, the seat belt retracting back in a rush, the metal fastener clanging against the door with a loud *thwap*. "Sorry," she whispers, but she doesn't stop her hurried movements, doesn't temper her obvious urge to get the hell out of the car.

"Brit—"

Her door slams.

And I know I should just wait here with the engine running, wait until she gets safely inside.

That I should then go home.

Go back to what we've been doing.

Separate. Better. *Safer.*

But I jab at the button on the dashboard, turn off the engine.

And open my door, walk up the path to the front door.

Then reach past her and push at the buttons on the keypad when I see her struggling with it like always, misclicking the buttons, forgetting to hit the pound sign, getting too impatient and making the lights flash as the lock resets.

Her gasp when my body comes close, when my hands brush hers away, is quiet, barely audible over the lock as I finish tapping the buttons and it *whirs* open.

I wrap my fingers around the handle, turn it, and shove the door open.

Now I should leave.

Instead, I move past her into the house.

She doesn't follow me, not for a long moment as I toe off my shoes, move down into the hall and into the kitchen. Eventually, though, I hear the sound of her footsteps on the floor, hear the door close, the lock *clicking* as it engages.

And then she's walking into the kitchen, looking like a fucking angel, so fucking beautiful it takes my breath away.

I inhale sharply, stomach twisting, bile in my throat.

She pauses by the sink, leans back against the counter, and... silence descends.

I expect her to break it.

I expect *me* to break it.

But it just stays there between us, a stifling, smothering blanket until I feel like I can't breathe.

And maybe that's why I do what I do next.

Maybe that's why I walk across the room, tug Brit into my arms...

Why I slant my lips over hers.

And feel like—for the first time in months—I can actually breathe.

TWELVE

BRIT

This is right.

This is everything as it should be.

Soft lips, a sleek tongue, the brush of a beard on my cheeks, my jaw, my chin.

A warm hand sliding up my back, wrapping around my nape, tilting my head back and tasting me deeper.

Slick darts of our tongues, my hands going to his shoulders, gripping tightly. His arm bands around my waist and one quick movement has me up onto the counter, the cold sinking through my leggings, chilling my skin.

But his body is hard and hot and that flash of discomfort is just that.

A flash.

There and gone until my body, my mind, my heart are solely focused on him.

On us.

Lips melding like they're one. All the hard of his body pressed to all the soft parts of mine. His fingers digging into my flesh, his scent surrounding me, his quiet groan vibrating across my tongue, skating over my breasts, fluttering across my belly, slipping between my thighs.

No.

That's not a groan slipping between my legs.

It's...his hand.

Sliding over my belly, dipping beneath the waistband of my leggings, my underwear.

Dancing over the thatch of short curls.

Parting slick folds and—

I gasp as he circles my clit, thighs clenching tightly around his waist, pelvis jerking, moan tumbling out of my mouth.

Because it's not just a circle, not just a teasing brush of touch.

He presses against that bundle of nerves, firmly, confidently, exactly as he knows I like it.

And then his thumb takes over on my clit, the rest of his fingers sliding down, one thick digit slipping inside.

"Oh!" I gasp, hips bucking. "Stef—"

But I don't finish rasping out his name because then his lips are back on mine and another finger is dipping into me, stretching me, the slight burn the perfect mix of pleasure and pain.

And already...it's building.

Flames of desire flickering between my thighs, catching fire in my stomach, beading my nipples into hard points that brush against my bra and send me shivering.

All the while, he's playing my body like an instrument, coiling pleasure in my clit, sending it out in wave after wave through my pussy, my thighs, my breasts...kissing me until I can't see straight, until I'm not certain I can draw in another breath, until one more touch is going to shatter me into a million pieces.

Only then does he slowly slide his lips from mine.

"Look at me, baby," he murmurs and I realize my eyes have slid shut. "Brit, sweetheart, let me see you."

"I'm close," I whisper, flutters beginning in my pussy, convulsing around his fingers.

"I know," he says softly before command slides into every

syllable of his next words. "Let me see you, baby."

I shudder when he presses hard at my clit, spine arching, head dropping back, a long moan escaping. "Stefan—"

Another press and I swear that my brain shuts down.

"Let. Me. See. You."

I'm a trembling mess. I can't feel my feet. My skin is too tight for my body. My mind is a haze of need and desire and—

"*Brit.*"

My lids peel back, eyes hitting the blazing blue of his.

"Come for me, baby," he orders softly.

And he presses that thumb.

And he thrusts those fingers.

And his mouth descends to cover mine again, tongue sliding between my lips, tangling with mine.

And—

I come.

Pleasure exploding out from my clit, my pussy convulsing around his fingers, tightening every muscle in my body, sending every nerve to high alert.

And then I'm falling apart, slumping down, elbows slamming onto the counter hard enough to steal the edge of my pleasure, to remind me of the always present pain in my side, the ache that never seems to go away.

Stefan curses, but then moves in a rush, hand coming behind my head, catching me before I bash my skull into the cabinets.

And the hurt in my torso fades as warmth covers me from head to toe at his show of care—old emotions and bliss, pleasure and the past all tangled up.

His fingers slide free of my pussy, sending aftershocks of my orgasm through my body.

And then I'm in his arms, cradled against his chest as he carries me through the kitchen, as he brings me up the stairs.

Down the hall.

Into our bedroom.

Onto our bed.

I reach for him as my body settles on the mattress, hands dropping onto his shoulders, fingers digging in, trying to draw him closer.

Only to feel him slip free of my hold.

My eyes shoot open.

And I watch as he takes a step back.

It's as though I'm smacked in the face with a freezing cold wave.

Or maybe that's just his eyes.

Blazing blue turned into frosty flecks of Arctic ice.

My throat is tight, but I manage to push out, "Stefan—"

Only to watch as he takes another step back.

His expression is frigid. Those eyes are ice. And all the while he's erecting the Grand Canyon between us.

"I—"

But now he's at the door, the light from the hall silhouetting his strong, muscular frame, the distance between us a never-ending gulf.

One second, I was in his arms.

The next, I'm cold and hurting and alone.

And that's what has my lips pressing together, what has my words stoppering up in the back of my throat. I'm not going to beg him to stay.

I've already done that.

And it didn't make one bit of difference.

He pauses, and I would be lying if I said that a blip of hope didn't bloom in my belly, my heart, my soul.

But that pause is a fraction of a second.

Then it's gone.

Just like him.

And then...

I'm alone.

Just like normal.

"Why?" I whisper once he's long gone. "Why did you stop loving me?"

THIRTEEN

STEFAN

"*Why did you stop loving me?*"

I heard those words all fucking night.

Interspersed with dreams about the slick heat of Brit's cunt, with the sounds of her moans, with the way she cried out my name.

A decade of her in my arms, my bed, my dreams.

But it was the first time those memories had become a nightmare.

I groan and shove myself out of bed, knowing that I slept for a collective hour, that I would likely feel more refreshed if I had just pulled an all-nighter like my (much) younger days.

Unfortunately, that's not what I did.

Unfortunately, I did a lot of dumb fucking things last night.

And I still have to meet my parents and Rox for breakfast at Molly's.

Something that will likely happen soon because my daughter is an early riser and my parents—my blissfully happily married parents (which is a mindfuck and a half)—are more than happy to oblige her in that.

I'll be getting a call within the hour to meet them.

And I'll be glad for it.

Because it's got to be better than sitting here and remembering what a fucking moron I am.

Remembering how much Brit has got to hate me.

Remembering—

I'm so lost in my own head that I almost miss the soft knock at the door.

But it catches on the edges of my hearing and it's enough for my swirling thoughts to halt for a moment, for relief to cascade through me.

I don't care if it's a former teammate or my parents back early to kidnap me for Molly's or a kid selling wrapping paper or someone trying to convince me that their newest type of carpet cleaner is the best.

It's a distraction from my dumbass brain, from my dumbass actions.

From...

My dumb *ass*.

I yank on a pair of sweats but don't bother with a shirt, just move down the hall and reach for the handle of the front door, pulling it open just as the person on the other side starts to knock again.

Which is how I find myself face-to-face with Tiffany.

My brows draw together. "Tiff? Is everything okay?"

She nods. "I—uh—I just realized I forgot my jacket and—"

I settle my hand on her shoulder. "Breathe," I order softly. "I have your jacket here." I nod toward the row of hooks mounted on the wall. "But...are you okay?"

"Yes," she says, gaze sliding away.

My gut twists. "Your mom?"

A shrug. "It's fine. *I'm* fine."

Spoiler alert: she's not fine.

"Sit down," I order softly, nudging her toward one of the chairs my mom bought years ago to decorate this porch. I'd teased her about them all the time when she lived here—accused her of wanting to keep an eye on the neighbors, all Karen-style. But the truth is that I liked sitting out here—probably more than she ever did—listening to the wind whistle through the trees that line the sidewalks, the kids playing at the park around the corner, the soft rumble of the odd car engine (or Amazon truck) coming down the quiet street.

"I'm fine," Tiff says again.

And, again, she's *not* fine.

Not fine at all.

So, I take her arm, draw her the rest of the way over to the chairs, gently push her down into one of them.

She doesn't fight me, just slumps against the wicker back, shoulders sagging, arms wrapping around herself.

"Stay," I mutter when she shivers, moving back toward the open door and snagging her coat from the hooks, bringing it back over to the chairs and wrapping it around her.

"Tell me," I command, albeit gently. "What's wrong, sweetheart?"

She shakes her head, grips her jacket so tightly her knuckles are turning bright white.

Then she starts to stand. "I should go—"

"Is it your mom?"

She stills.

But only for a second.

Because then her expression crumples—face going pale, bottom lip trembling, eyes filling with tears.

One of which escapes, clinging to thick dark brown lashes for a single taut moment before dropping onto her pallid skin, sliding down her cheek, dripping off the curve of her jaw.

Shit.

She turns away, starts for the stairs that lead off the porch. "I'll see you later—"

I snag her arm. "Tiff."

A sob hitches through her torso and I turn her back to face

me, heart squeezing hard at the sight of more tears streaking down her cheeks, the shining tracks of her pain blatantly obvious in the warm fall sunshine. "I'm fine—"

"Bullshit." I wrap my arms around her, tug her into a tight hug when she tries to pull away. "You're not fine." A beat. "Tell me."

Stiff like a statue.

Then she exhales, drops her hands to her sides, and...she lets go.

Sobs hitching her chest, tears dripping down my skin, body shaking so hard that it seems as though she is going to shatter into a thousand pieces. I hold her tighter, rub a hand up and down her spine. "Shh," I say softly. "It's okay. Let it out, sweetheart. Just take a breath and let it out."

And she does.

Those tears not slowing. Those sobs not stopping.

That shaking going on and on and on.

It's unbearable, but I don't tell her to stop.

I just stand there and let her give it to me.

Eventually, her tears slow and she pushes lightly at my chest. I let her draw back, but don't completely release her.

"I'm sorry," she murmurs so softly I have to lean in to hear her. "I didn't come here for this. I—"

I cup her jaw, tilt her head up, and meet those tear-swollen eyes. "You're family, sweetheart. If you can't come here for a hug, then—"

A flicker of movement catches my attention and I barely hear Tiff say, "I should be able to handle my mom's bullshit by now."

Because it's not just movement, not a bird or a squirrel or a neighbor walking their dog.

It's...

Brit.

My gaze hits my ex-wife's, and it only takes a heartbeat for the hurt in her chocolate-brown eyes to eviscerate me.

But even before I can drop my arms from Tiff, can step back, can apologize for being such a dumbfuck the night before, she's turned, hustled down the driveway and gotten into her car.

The tires squeal as she pulls away from the curb.

Tiff's expression is grave as I manage to tear my eyes from Brit's car disappearing and look back down at her.

"I should go," she whispers.

"Tiff," I say. "It's—"

A shake of her head.

A harder push against my chest.

And just like I'm good at, just like I'm best at...

I let her go.

Fourteen

Brit

It takes every part of me to slow down, to drive safely, to watch out for the kids playing at the park. But I manage to regain control. To watch out for animals as I turn the corner. To keep my eyes peeled and make sure a ball followed by a tiny human doesn't careen out in front of me. I let off the gas, make sure I go precisely the speed limit, and clear that hurdle.

And then carefully make my way out of the rest of the neighborhood.

And onto the freeway.

Only once I'm cruising along do I finally breathe, my exhale loud enough to startle me.

To remind myself that I'm sitting in silence, clenching the steering wheel and my teeth in turn.

I deliberately relax my jaw, loosen my grip, and roll out my shoulders.

And then I'm reliving the moment of walking up the driveway of Stefan's place after being up all night (because I sure as shit hadn't been able to sleep after what had happened between us).

But somewhere around five in the morning, I'd started to think, to wonder, to *hope*...

Maybe this was the start of something different. That maybe we couldn't go back, but maybe we could...

Have something different.

Something new.

Something...better.

And *that* was the emotion I'd driven to Stefan's house with. My heart pulsing, hope blooming, words already jumbled as they bounced around my mind.

Because my stupid, *stupid* brain is an asshole.

Because I'd been so wrapped up in my idiotic hope that I'd missed Stefan on the porch.

With Tiffany in his arms.

"God," I groan, head dropping back for a second.

Not long enough to crash, considering the highway is cooking along this early in the morning.

Though I can't lie.

I'm tempted to just veer a little to the left, to let my car just do a little smooshy-smoosh into the center divide.

If it wouldn't kill me and take me from Roxie, wouldn't potentially hurt someone else, I might actually skip beyond intrusive thoughts and plummet straight into—

Well, that center divide.

Thankfully, I have a kid to live for.

And a hockey team.

And...myself, no matter how much I'm slowly dying inside.

Normally, when I feel like this, I would go spend time with my girl.

But it's not my custody time, and I know all about her sleepover with Stefan's parents. And...I know they would welcome me, would include me (they always have, and have made it a point to continue doing so through the shitshow that's been Stefan and my breakup). But I also know that I definitely cannot see Diane, can't see Pierre.

Not with how I'm feeling right now.

They will see right the fuck through me.

And...

Yeah, I've seen enough pitying looks over the last months to be desperate to avoid more.

I could go for a run—

I shudder, remembering grubby hands on me and lips that were all wrong.

A run. Sure.

Because the last one went so well.

I flick on my signal, navigate to the off-ramp.

Because, really, I've only got one safe space to go.

It's likely why my subconscious sent me in this direction even before I came out of my panic.

It's familiar.

It's comfortable.

It's...all I've got left.

I maneuver through the signals, navigate over to the practice rink, and use my keycard to access the hallway that leads to the locker room less than ten minutes later.

My equipment is here and not at the Gold Mine (the arena where the Gold play our home games), thankfully. Set out and ready for practice later today.

I always have a backup set here, but they're not the ones I wear for our games because my leg pads get worn in so quickly that they are the one piece of equipment that goes back and forth between the practice facility and the arena.

And get changed out every two months or so.

Way more often than my lucky glove that's been with me for the entire season.

Never let it be said that hockey players aren't superstitious.

I strip out of my clothes, pull on my gear, and am tying on my pads when I sense movement in the open door.

"I knew you'd be here," Frankie says.

Our long-time goaltending coach has been a staple in my life for as long as I've been playing in the league, and the sight of him is almost enough for my eyes to tear up.

Luckily, I'm good at holding that shit in as I look up at him and smile. "How'd you know?"

He grins. "That you'd want to get beat up with some pucks shot by an old man?"

"Yes," I say with real amusement this time. "Exactly that."

He winks. "Because I know you." He tilts his head in the direction of the ice. "I'll go get those pucks."

My heart squeezes and I nod. "Thanks, Frankie."

"Are you kidding?" he says, pushing off the doorframe and stepping back into the hall. "The wife is more than happy to get me out of the house. Plus"—he flexes his biceps, wags his brows—"she likes the guns it gives me."

I snort, mostly because if there's anything similar about all hockey goalies (besides being more than a little weird for willingly standing in front of a goal and getting hard-ass disks of rubber shot at us), it's that we're all on the leaner side. Tall and lean.

And without huge biceps.

Though technically I'm short when compared to some of the behemoths manning the league's other nets—even though I'm tall for a woman. Biology is a fact I can't compete with and something I've had to learn to compensate for.

Hence the extra practice.

Hence the ability to forget about my life by having to focus on those hockey pucks.

I exhale, finish with the last tie, check the buckles, and then I put on my chest protector, my jersey, my helmet. I snag my glove and blocker, my stick from the rack just outside the door.

Then I'm moving down the hall, feeling the cool kiss of the arena's icy air on my cheeks.

Colder as I approach the opening to the rink, clinging to my skin, soaking in through my jersey. Cool and damp and with the faint undertones of the propane they use to fuel the Zamboni that was just out here, smoothing the ice for me, making sure the surface is clear of snow and divots.

I hear the crunch of Frankie's skates, the crack of his stick, the *plink* as a puck hits a post.

Another thud, this time the harder, more solid sound of it hitting the boards. And again, this time a higher pitch *clang* as it ricochets off the glass.

Fast, even for my awesome goalie coach, and I realize why when I clear the opening, when I see my former teammate, Rome, out on the ice, along with Josh and Will and Lucas. The three Musketeers and our wayward charge, lately traded across the bay to the Oakland Eagles.

Life throwing him a curveball, forcing him to start over and hating the process every step of the way.

Losing his family (though we'll never let him go).

But...

I feel what he's feeling.

Or *felt*, anyway.

Because now he's thriving, making a name for himself as their newest captain (and love interest of the intrepid and more than a little scary owner of the Eagles' daughter).

He's also the first one to spot me, skating over, snagging a sip from a water bottle tucked onto the shelf of the bench, his eyes locking with mine. "You're a mess," he says softly.

"Well, it's so lovely to see you too, Rome," I return, going for light.

And having the feeling that I'm failing completely because his face gentles further, his voice goes even softer, and he settles an arm around my shoulders. "Fucking hell, Banana-rama."

I pull it together.

Because I'm good at that.

"Have I told you how much I hate that nickname?" I mock grumble.

His mouth kicks up. "Have you forgotten that once a team

assigns you a nickname, there's nothing to be done but to take it?"

Words I've said a hundred, if not a thousand times before.

"Well, *fine*, my little Romeo."

He winces, but to his credit, doesn't complain. Just hitches his head toward the ice. "So, do you want to get some shots in? Or not?"

"Is my name not Brit Plantain Barie?" I tease.

Then I remember.

I'm *not* Brit Plantain Barie any longer.

I'm just...Brit Plantain.

FIFTEEN

STEFAN

She still moves like lightning, sliding across the crease in a flash of movement, stopping pucks she shouldn't be able to stop, especially considering how old she is, how hurt she'd been a year ago, how—

For all intents and purposes, her career should be over.

For another player, it likely would be.

And yet, she persists.

Not being dragged along behind the team either.

Strong, carrying *them* through games at times, and though she's not the clear starter any longer—the team allowing her to share the role and give their former backup plenty of game time to gain experience—she's still that solid presence the Gold needs.

Just like she was *my* solid presence.

Until she wasn't.

I sigh, push off the wall, start to turn for the exit.

I've gotten the call, know that my parents and Rox are heading to Molly's.

It's time for hot cocoa with extra whipped cream and pastries that are flakey and yummy and delicious, and—

"What are you doing to our girl?"

I stop in the face of two women with stern expressions and crossed arms. Though it was the little one who had spoken, I know they are both dangerous and deadly, especially in protection of one they love.

I raise my hands, palms out. "I don't interfere in your guys' relationships—"

This sends Mandy—the taller of the duo and head trainer for the Gold—snorting, her brows lifting. "You mean you didn't interfere when Blane tried to tell me that insider VIP passes to a certain boy wizard's theme park experience were too expensive?"

I shake my head. "That's different. You love the little scarred bastard and it was only available for a limited time."

Her brows flick higher. "And it wasn't interference when I was ready to take up arms when he wanted to take my little Maddy in the ocean"—a beat—"with *sharks* and you talked me down from the edge?"

I shrug. "The chances of a shark attack are—"

She shudders and waves a hand. "Don't." A breath, expression clearing, hardening. "My point is that we are who we are, and that means we interfere in each other's lives because we love each other, and it *means*"—she juts out her chin in irritation—"that when someone is being dumb, we call them on their bullshit."

I clench my back teeth together, exhale, then turn toward Sara. "You going to let her do the talking?"

One slender shoulder lifts and falls. "Mandy's doing great all on her own."

Great at making that guilt—ever-present inside me—grow and swell until it feels like I can barely draw in air.

"It's all over the news," Mandy says and I return my focus to her, heart sinking.

"What's all over the news?" I ask, even though my heart is sinking.

"That you've officially filed for divorce."

My eyes slide closed.

Fuck.

Silence for a beat before Sara takes over. "Now that the season's underway, the story's been picked up nationally." She shakes her head. "The headline in the *Times* this morning is: *Hockey's Power Couple is Splitsville. Female Goalie Can't Stop This. Plantain is Barie No More.*"

I shudder.

God, the media are just a bunch of assholes.

And not even fucking creative.

Dumbasses.

I sigh, shove down the surge of protectiveness that wants to send me back toward Brit, that wants to shelter her from this shit. I want to track down every newspaper and throw them into a bonfire. I want to crash every website carrying the story, torpedo their apps.

But...

I don't.

Because I can't go back.

Because I had to do it.

Because it was for her own good. The news will blow over and—

"Do you really not care?" Mandy snaps. "That you've shredded her through and through?"

My throat goes tight. "I—"

"Mom!"

We all turn, see that Mandy's oldest, Maddy, is running toward us.

Freeing me from the hot seat.

Putting this fucking conversation to rest.

But not making the guilt go away.

I inhale, exhale, hold myself still through the battering ram of that remorse, pull it together enough to say a proper hello to Maddy, to exchange a terse goodbye with Mandy. But Sara hangs back as the pair goes to get ready for the skating lesson Sara is giving Maddy that morning, and I know that all of the bracing

I'm doing isn't going to be enough for the blow that's about to fly my way.

"She thinks that she wasn't woman enough for you."

I freeze, having to clench every muscle in my body to stop myself from crumpling over.

Because Brit thinks—

And last night—

And this morning—

And—

Fucking hell.

"Yeah," Sara mutters. "I figured that might finally get through your big, dumb brain."

"I—"

She lifts a hand. "I don't want to hear it. I don't know what's going on with you two, haven't been in your bedroom other than to help my girl pick out an outfit so someone might think she's attractive and sexy and *wanted*."

One blow after another.

Bam. Bam. Bam.

"So, no, I understand that I don't get every nuance of your guys' lives," she murmurs. "But I've been around enough to know when someone I love is fucking up royally."

She turns away.

Turns back.

"And, just to clarify, the person who's fucking up is you," she says. Half of her mouth curves. "In case there's any doubt of that."

There's not any doubt.

None whatsoever.

But I still suck in a breath, try to formulate a response that can justify why I've done what I've done without revealing *why* the fuck I've done what I've done.

Turns out that I don't need to come up with an excuse.

Because Sara is turning away again, only this time she doesn't rotate back to mentally jab at me. She walks away, leaving me standing there like an idiot.

Or an asshole who's likely made the biggest mistake of his life...

An asshole who can't do shit about it, even if I want to.

A puck cracks against the glass, and my gaze is drawn over my shoulder, drawn toward the rink and the players on it. Drawn toward the woman who's manning the net like she's been born to it.

Probably because she *was* born to it.

Playing this sport like it's in her blood, her heart, her soul.

Because it is.

Our eyes connect, chocolate brown with my own blue, and I feel my pulse pick up, rattling through my veins.

Holding.

Staring.

Wishing things could be different.

But knowing they can't be.

"This is how it has to be," I whisper.

But as I stand there, staring into milk chocolate eyes I know better than my own, I wonder...

Is it truly the way it has to be?

Sixteen

BRIT

"Mom?"

The door squeaks open and I barely hold back my groan.

I flick my gaze to the clock on my bedside table, see that I've been in bed, trying to sleep, for barely any time at all.

Away game. Flight. Back to the practice facility on the bus to pick up my car. Then to the house, checking on Rox, relieving Diane who was watching her, and finally stumbling up to my room, collapsing into bed, and...

Laying here with my eyes closed for all of twenty-four minutes.

"Mom?" Rox asks again, light creeping into my room.

I sit up, flick on the bedside lamp. "I'm awake, baby. What's the matter?"

She'd looked a little flushed when I checked on her earlier, and Diane mentioned she had a tummy ache.

I really hope that wasn't the start of food poisoning or the stomach flu.

A special brand of hell, cleaning up your kids' vomit when you have no fucking sleep.

"I don't feel good."

I know that tone, know what the color of Roxie's skin means.

The wrong side of pale but with bright pink cheeks.

Fever and—

I toss the blankets back, swing my legs out of bed, feet hitting the carpet a bare second later.

But it's still too late.

Roxie's little body tenses—

And then she pukes all over the floor.

I rush over to her, ignoring her when she tries to apologize, when she starts to cry, swooping her up into my arms, holding her close as we race into the bathroom, hurry toward the toilet.

I plunk her down onto the rug in front of it, reach for her hair and hold it back as she continues to retch.

"I'm—" Cough. "Sorry—"

"Shh, baby," I tell her, stroking a hand up and down her back. "Don't worry about it. Just get everything out, honey." I place a hand over her forehead, feel that her skin is blazing hot.

Damn.

Not food poisoning then.

Likely a stomach flu.

Which means that *I'm* probably going to get the stomach flu.

And maybe Diane too.

Great.

I'll have to text her a warning in a bit, advise that she take a bath in hand sanitizer.

Kids.

Fun times.

The little germ machines.

"My tummy hurts, Mommy," she whispers when she finally stops puking, and my heart squeezes tightly at the use of *Mommy*. I've been straight *Mom* for a while now and had mourned the loss of my baby growing up.

That she's using it now?

My soul can't take it.

But I have to.

"What kind of stomachache do you have?" I ask. "The kind that your food isn't agreeing with you? Or that you need to sit on the toilet?"

"Uh-uh."

I open my mouth to ask her which question that *uh-uh* answered, but I don't get the chance.

Because she's puking again, heaving until nothing is coming up, and then shivering in my arms when I cuddle her close.

Fevers and chills.

Damn.

"You think you're done, baby?"

A teeth-chattering nod.

I scoop her up again, carry her to my bed, and tuck her under the blankets. "I'll be right back, baby girl," I murmur, brushing her sweaty bangs off her forehead.

Fatigue clings to my limbs as I hurry back into the bathroom, wet a cloth, snag a trash can, then hurry over to her and drape it over her blazing skin, strategically positioning the garbage pail to catch anything that might come up while I'm cleaning up.

I know I need to get something in her to help with the fever, but it's too soon, I think, for her to keep anything down. So instead, I grab the carpet spray and some paper towels, start scrubbing at the spot on the floor.

Holding back my gags at the smell and trying not to get anything on my hands as I scrub accompanies my next five minutes, but eventually the carpet is clean—or as clean as it will be. I set the spray on the shelf, get rid of the dirty paper towels, and—

Hear it as I walk back into the bedroom door.

More retching.

"Shit," I whisper, hurrying over to Rox, placing my hand on

her forehead, feeling that she's even hotter than she was ten minutes before.

I grab the thermometer, manage to get a temperature, and—

Freeze.

One-oh-five.

"Dammit," I whisper.

But I can't get the Tylenol, can't hurry to the bathroom and run the cloth under cool water again.

Because she starts puking.

And the temperature I retake when she stops hasn't gone down.

"It hurts, Mommy," she says, clutching her tummy, tears rolling down her cheeks. "It really, *really* hurts."

Panic eats at the back of my throat, my heart is thudding hard against my rib cage, my hands shake and I feel more than a little sick myself.

Because I don't know what's wrong.

I just know that something *is* wrong.

"Hang on, baby," I murmur. "Just hang on."

I grab clothes and yank them on, shove my feet into shoes, tie back my hair and snag a jacket, a phone charger, and my cell. Then I'm down the hall, rushing into Roxie's room, grabbing her unicorn tote, shoving a blanket inside, along with socks and clothes and shoes.

"Breathe, Brit," I whisper, spinning in a circle, looking around, trying to think of something else my baby might need.

My gaze lands on a well-worn stuffed tabby cat, one eye missing, the fur matted and clearly on the wrong side of loved.

Battered and stitched together.

But Rox still loves Mr. Fluffernut.

I snag him, shove him in as well, and then haul ass back down to the bedroom, back to my baby. "Come on, love," I murmur.

She groans as I lift her.

"It's okay," I promise. "I'm going to make it okay."

SEVENTEEN

STEFAN

My phone rings and I drag my lids back.

I immediately know it's the middle of the night.

My body has never lost the skill to deal with all manner of lack of sleep and shoot instantly awake, aware of my surroundings and the time and ready to tackle any situation—

Or to play hockey anyway.

Not the most useful skill.

But it's *some* skill.

And it helped with those late nights waiting for Brit, helped with Rox when she was a baby who didn't want to sleep, and a toddler...who didn't want to sleep.

And a young kid...

Who didn't want to sleep.

Buzz-buzz.

I shake myself out of my thoughts, turn toward my nightstand, and snag my cell off the charger.

My heart squeezes when I see the name on the screen.

Brit.

Brit is calling me.

Which is unusual enough, especially when she's been keeping a careful distance between us the last couple of weeks. The wall she deliberately threw up thick and impenetrable and...

Exactly what needed to be in place.

But now Brit is calling me.

And she's doing it in the middle of the night.

"Fuck," I mutter, shaking my head to get it the fuck together then swiping my finger across the screen, lifting it up to my ear. "Hello?"

There's a long pause.

But not a silent one.

Noise in the background—voices and clanking, clicking, strange noises that part of me feels like I should know, but can't place. Not at this moment. Not when my mind is spinning and my pulse is pounding and worry is clawing at my insides.

"Brit?" I say. "Are you there?"

Another pause, but thankfully this one is broken by a breath rattling through the speakers, the sound sharp and loud enough to send me upright.

"*Brit.*"

One more breath, but thank fuck she starts to talk. "I got home and was sleeping and Roxie came in saying she wasn't feeling well." This wasn't abnormal. Our daughter had been having plenty of *sick* days since we separated.

Needing the extra attention and comfort...

And to take up the bulk of our respective beds she conned her way into sharing.

That's normal.

The rest of what Brit tells me isn't.

"Your mom mentioned she might not be feeling well, that she'd had a stomachache and didn't eat dinner." Another breath. "I just figured it was normal kid stuff. But then she started puking and had a fever and said her stomach hurt really, *really* bad. I was worried, but not too much because she's a kid and kids get sick and—"

Her voice trembles.

My heart squeezes hard. "Brit, sweetheart—"

"And she *kept* puking," she blurts out. "And was *so* hot. I took her temperature and it was a hundred-and-five—"

I jolt.

Because Roxie's been sick before.

But not with a fever that high.

"And she was hurting, and I didn't know what to do, so I bundled her up and drove her to the hospital and—"

The noise rises in the background.

But before I can order Brit to go on, the din quiets and she starts talking again as I get out of bed and move to my dresser, start yanking out clothes, pulling them on. "—and they're not exactly sure what's going on still, but they've given her something for her fever and the pain and they're sending her to get a CT scan to check her appendix and—" Her voice hitches again before the volume decreases. "—she might have to have emergency surgery, hon—"

An exhale.

The endearment cut off in the tracks.

"She might have to have emergency surgery, Stefan—"

A razor blade over my skin. A knife to the kidneys. A lance between my ribs.

"—and I thought you should know," she says, her tone even now. The panic faded. The worry carefully hidden and banked. "I know it's not your custody time, but she's asking for you. But you don't have to come—"

"Brit."

"—I just thought you should know what's going on and—"

"*Brit.*"

"—I should go, let you get back to sleep—"

"Shut up, sweetheart."

She inhales, that air rattling my cell's speaker again.

Another endearment.

Fucking stupid.

Emotions—*mine*—barreling through the wall she erected like the Kool-Aid Man.

"I—"

"What hospital are you two at?" I blurt out before she can tell me to shut the fuck up, to stop being a goddamn idiot.

She tells me. "But you don't have to come—"

"I'll be there."

Another breath rattling through my ears.

"Hang on, sweetheart," I tell her. "I'll be there as soon as I can."

A long pause. "But you—"

"I'll be there soon, baby."

"I—"

"Bye."

"I—"

I hang up, yank on a hoodie, grab my shoes, step into them.

Into the hall.

Keys off the hook in the kitchen, moving into the garage, hitting the button to open the heavy metal door. I fold myself into the driver's seat, turn on the ignition, back out of the driveway, pull onto the street.

Navigating the dark and quiet highway.

Pulling into the hospital parking lot.

Moving into the ER waiting room, speaking with the registrar.

And finally—

Fucking *finally*.

—making my way back to the patient rooms.

Making my way back to the two people who own my soul.

Even though it really should just be one.

Because the woman I see, her expression drawn, her hair pulled sharply back from her face, dark circles beneath her eyes, skin beyond pale, shouldn't make my heart roll over in my chest, shouldn't make me have to clench my jaw, draw my hands into fists, dig my toes into the soles of my shoes just to resist the urge to pull her into my arms and promise that everything will be okay.

I force my body to relax, tamp down the instinct to draw Brit close.

And I move to Roxie's bedside.

But every cell in my body remains focused on my ex-wife.

Eighteen

Brit

Roxie's finally sleeping, her temperature having begun to creep down, her pain under control when Stefan shows up in the doorway, one of the nurses drawing the curtain to the side after apparently guiding him to us.

He stops in the opening, big body stilling like a gorgeous god-like statue.

A muscle in his cheek flickers and his hands clench into fists.

And he stands like that for one long moment.

Then his head turns to the side, his gaze collides with mine, and I suck in a breath, half expecting him to come toward me, to draw me close and reassure me that our baby is going to be okay.

And I swear I can actually feel his hug, feel his arms coming around me, feel the hard muscles of his chest and the warmth of his body sinking in through my clothes. Smell the spice of his scent and—

He starts moving.

My pulse leaps.

Hope blooms...

And is extinguished as he rounds the bed, putting it between us, his attention completely on our sick daughter.

As it should be, you fucking egomaniac.

Guilt pours into the wound in my heart, burning like it's salt water, but I grind my teeth, push it down, and focus on what I should.

What I need to.

Roxie.

"They gave her something to sleep," I say. "She was in a lot of pain and they're waiting for CT to come down and take her."

His eyes flick to mine and he nods, smooths back her hair. "Do they know how long that will be?"

I shake my head. "They want to get her in as quickly as possible, but who knows how long that'll take."

Another nod, but his focus is Roxie. "She still puking?"

"No." I clear my throat. "They gave her something for that too."

"Good," he murmurs.

And then, because there's nothing else to do besides wait, I sit down in the chair I pulled up next to the bed, and...I wait.

Wait as my head slumps forward and my eyelids grow heavy from the lack of sleep.

Wait as the only sounds that fill the room are Roxie's even breathing, the noise from the hall, from other patients—a baby crying, a parent soothing, nurses and doctors talking.

But not Stefan and me.

Nope.

No fucking way.

We're just silently ignoring each other for absolutely no reason—and really, after more than a decade, you would think that we'd have something to say to each other.

Alas...not so much.

What do I say to an ex-husband who dislikes me enough to divorce me but then beats up my date (rightfully—and as much as it pains me to admit—thankfully so)? Oh, yeah, and then he finger fucks me until I come so hard I can barely move before he dumps me on my bed then leaves.

And I spend the night wondering and thinking and not sleeping and...

Hoping.

Before I go over early in the morning, that hope still growing, blooming into something fragile and beautiful and—

Easily destroyed.

Like, say, when I stumble upon my husband with a woman who's beautiful and nice and younger than me, a woman who's more of a woman than I'll ever be, a woman who—

Left me with absolutely no question about where I stand.

Because he's my fucking *ex*-husband.

Something I need to remember on the fucked-up merry-go-round that's my head.

I bite the inside of my cheek. Hold in my groan...

And the urge to bang my head against the wall.

And then I deliberately push the thoughts out of my head, deliberately stop thinking about everything to do with Stefan, with me, with our painful past and fucked-up present.

I'm a good mom.

I can continue with that, can focus on that, can—

The knock has me jerking upright, realizing that somehow I've fallen asleep. My neck and back and side hate me, but I'm not focused on my screaming and seizing muscles, not when I realize I've pushed myself to sitting off a pillow that has somehow materialized beneath my face.

With all of my magical skills.

Right. And their name is Stefan.

My *ex*-husband.

I internally shake my head then exhale, push the pillow from my mind (along with the one person—*man*—who could have put it there), and turn toward the woman in the lab coat walking our direction. "I'm here to take Roxie up to CT. Which one of you guys is coming with me?" she asks, glancing down at her clipboard. "The other will just need to hang out here. It won't be long."

I nod, push up to my feet, intending to follow.

But Roxie is awake.

And she breaks my heart—though not with any ill intent.

Just with the childlike innocence of her saying,

"I want Dad."

I freeze, eyes shifting to the bed, to the woman who's set down her clipboard and is now fiddling with the controls on the bed, unlocking the brake, then over to Stefan who's holding as still as I am.

And finally, to Roxie, who's hurting and scared and wants her dad.

"Of course, baby," I say, stroking a hand over her forehead, bending and pressing a quick kiss there. She's still running a fever, still unwell.

So, I step back.

"I'll take good care of her," the woman says, pushing the bed forward, rolling it toward the door, Stefan trailing behind.

"I know you both will," I murmur, thighs trembling, having to lock my knees as I watch them go.

Stefan glances over his shoulder as he turns the corner, his pale blue eyes connecting with mine.

I suck in a breath.

My legs threaten to give way.

But I hold it together as he pulls his gaze from mine and follows Roxie.

Only then do I give in and allow my knees to buckle, my ass to hit the thin padding of the hospital-grade chair, the tears in my eyes to well up and over my lashes, to drip down my cheeks.

But I don't let them fall for long.

I don't want my baby girl to see that I'm upset.

So, I relieve the pressure, suck in several deep breaths, blowing them out so fucking slowly that I feel as though I'm going to pass out. But fear of losing consciousness means that I regain enough control to stifle the sobs, to dash the backs of my hands across my cheeks, to dry the tears.

And it means that by the time Roxie is wheeled back into the little room that's become our sad little home for these early hours of dawn, there's not a trace of my moment of weakness.

But why do I have the feeling that Stefan sees it anyway?

Nineteen

Stefan

The tech clicks her tongue as she looks at the screen and sighs.

"What?" I ask, leaning in, trying to make heads or tails of the grayscale images of my daughter's insides.

"I can't read them," she says, nodding to the screens. "The radiologist has to do that, but if I was a betting woman, I'd say that appendix needs to come out, and come out soon."

Surgery.

My little girl was going to have surgery.

Christ.

That unleashes a tendril of fear in me like no other.

"Breathe," the woman says, clamping a hand onto my shoulder. "You're here, which is exactly where you need to be."

I nod, take that breath she advises.

"Good," she tells me before dropping her hand and clicking the mouse, tapping at the keyboard. "Okay, it's off to the radiologist, let's get you two back to your wife—"

"Ex-wife," I correct instinctively.

Instinctively...but completely unnecessarily.

"Right," she says, clearing her throat. "Let's...um...get you two back."

I nod woodenly but manage to not make myself sound like more of a douchebag as we walk back into the room and help Rox back onto the gurney. I stride silently beside them on the way back down to the ER.

It takes just one glimpse of Brit sitting in the chair, shoulders stiff, but posture so fragile to know that the smallest shove will send her toppling to the ground, shattering into a million pieces.

She smiles—a blisteringly fake one—when we walk back into the room, and moves over to Roxie, gently taking her hand.

"Hi, Mom," Rox says quietly.

And that right there would be enough for us to know that something is seriously wrong with our daughter. She's never quiet. She's never still.

"Hey, baby girl," Brit whispers. "We're going to get you all sorted, okay? You'll be feeling better in no time."

"Okay," Rox murmurs, lids drooping.

"Rest now, sweetheart. Your dad and I have you."

Roxie's eyes slide closed, but her lips curve up, and she gives a slight nod before slipping off into sleep.

"What is it?" Brit asks, pushing up from her chair with a wince and moving over to my side.

I tilt my head for the hall, not wanting little ears to hear something they shouldn't, not until we're certain, and when we're out of range, I quietly relay the information.

Brit bites her lip. "But how long will it take for someone to tell us if she needs surgery—?"

She doesn't get the chance to finish that statement because the doctor walks up, expression serious.

And just like that, our baby is getting prepped for surgery.

It all happens in a rush.

One second we're in the ER, Roxie having just drifted off to sleep, and the next we're being bundled off to a room and my daughter is awake and scared and in pain and doesn't want us to leave her.

She clings to Brit's hand, all in on her mom right now. "I don't want to, Mom. Please don't make me."

The nurse is working on her IV, getting ready to administer some happy juice—a.k.a. something to relax her. But it's not in Rox's body right now and that switch inside her has been triggered.

There's no pulling her back from the edge.

Not when she gets like this.

It's why her threenager years were fucking torture.

"Rox, baby," Brit says, cupping her face in both hands. "Sometimes we have to do things we really don't like to do. Remember with the IV"—she nods at Rox's arm—"you didn't want to have the needle when we first came in, right? But you did it and they made you feel better and—"

"I do feel better," Rox says, clearly grasping at straws. "I'm *all* better, so I don't need to—"

"A slight sting, honey," the nurse murmurs. Not that Roxie hears. She's too focused on Brit and proving that she's better, that her appendix isn't at risk of bursting.

Not that she knows what that means.

Roxie hisses.

Brit keeps her face close, keeps her focus.

Distraction is key sometimes.

"I know you're feeling better, but they're going to help you feel even *more* better," she says, tone light and easy. "So much so that you'll be back on the ice and can do sleepovers at Uncle Mike and Auntie Sara's place in no time."

Roxie's face is relaxing, but I can tell she hasn't bought in, not completely anyway.

"And we can go down to Half Moon Bay," Brit says, "and have one of our special Mom Dates."

Rox's lids—which had been slowly sliding closed—flash open. "To the fancy hotel by the ocean?"

Brit's mouth hitches up. "Yeah, baby."

"Another sting, sweetie," the nurse says.

Roxie winces. "Can we get pedicures, Mom?"

Brit chuckles softly. "Always negotiating, huh, baby girl?"

"It's my superpower," Rox announces proudly, though the words are more than a little slurred now.

Brit chuckles again. "Yes to brunch and pedicures," she says, then gently nudges Roxie back onto the gurney. "Now relax, baby, and let us worry about you for a bit."

"That's *your* superpower," Rox murmurs, lids shutting.

And bribery for the win.

"Nice, Mama," the nurse whispers, hanging an IV bag onto the machine next to Roxie's and then bending down to unlock the brakes. "We'll have her back to you safe and sound as soon as possible."

"Thanks," Brit says so softly I barely hear it.

But maybe that's because she's already backing away, already heading for the door out into the hallway. Not waiting like I am, waiting as they wheel Rox through another set of doors that will lead to the operating room, waiting until our daughter is fully out of sight.

I swallow against the rise of emotion then turn and go out into the hall, starting for the waiting room they showed us earlier.

But a noise has me stopping in my tracks.

Rotating to the right.

And finding Brit tucked back into an alcove, curled into a ball, face pressed to her knees, shoulders shaking with tears.

"Sweetheart," I whisper.

She stiffens, quiets.

Then turns her face away from me as she scrubs her hands over it.

She straightens, glances my way—though she does it without her eyes meeting mine—and then she starts walking down the hall, walking away from me.

I should let her go.

But...

Our baby is in the operating room.

So, I catch her arm as she tries to brush by me.

"I'm fine," she says, trying to pull out of my grasp.

I ignore her, draw her back against my chest, folding her in my arms.

Holding her close until she does what she needs to—

Lets it all come out.

TWENTY

BRIT

"Can I have the Jell-O now, Mom?"

I blink, shake off the sleep, and smile at my baby girl.

We've progressed from juice (clear liquids) to solids (the strawberry-flavored Jell-O my munchkin is currently eyeing up). "Of course, peanut," I say, peeling open the foil lid, snagging a spoon, and passing both over. "Slowly," I warn when she goes full Gollum *my precious* and downs half of it in just a couple of mouthfuls.

She slows down.

Marginally.

But that's my Roxie—always going at full speed.

Even apparently when it comes to surgery recovery.

We'll be out of here in a few hours—as long as this Jell-O stays down and nothing concerning happens over the next little while.

Which is a good thing.

Because I need to sleep for a hundred years.

Unfortunately, I have a game tonight.

One I know the team—considering the owner is Rox's grandpa—wouldn't have a problem with me missing.

But...

I can use the space.

Because Stefan is going to stay at my house. In the guest bedroom.

I grind my teeth together.

It's good for Roxie to have him close.

It's fine. It's great.

But...I'd really like to get out of the house for a couple of hours if I can manage it.

Stefan's phone rings, but I don't look at him as he answers it.

I sure as shit hear him say, "Hey, Tiff," though.

My heart convulses, but I just straighten Roxie's blanket, force my attention to the phone in her lap that's playing some stupid unboxing video that Rox is obsessed with.

"Yeah, that sounds good, but we're only supposed to be here for a couple more hours," he says. "Want to meet us at Brit's place? I'm sure Rox would love to see you when she gets settled."

Inviting his girlfriend to my house.

Without asking me. Without so much as glancing in my direction and lifting a brow in query.

Just—

Well, come on in, gorgeous, younger woman who's way better than me in so many—MANY—ways. Did you know that in addition to me being a jealous bitch, I also participated—willingly—in cheating on you when Stefan finger fucked me on this countertop not that long ago? Don't worry, though, I carefully sanitized everything. Now, can I make you a cup of coffee?

My throat closes up and I clench my teeth together, barely able to stopper up those words.

Luckily, I do. Luckily, I'm focused on that stupid video so I can't look over at Stefan and reveal the turmoil in my belly, my soul.

Because this isn't me.

I'm not a woman who's with a cheater.

I'm not a woman who pines after a man who cheats and then goes right back home to his woman.

I'm not a woman who denigrates myself, who cuts myself down, who compares myself to others.

That. Is. *Not*. Me.

And I've been in this state of torment for too damned long.

Enough is enough already.

Stefan's staying in the guest room—great, that means Roxie can be comfortable and not have to go house to house.

Tiffany is coming over—also great because Roxie loves her and the more people who love my daughter, the better.

I'm...going to be there. With them.

Pain lances through me, but I inhale silently through my nose, hold it long enough for my lungs to protest, then let it slide out of my mouth just as soundlessly.

Then I put the bitterness and hurt aside.

I don't shove it down, not like before.

It's...placed to the side. There and palpable and I'm aware of it. Not ignoring. Not pretending it doesn't exist.

That's a lesson in futility.

The feelings are real.

And I'm acknowledging them.

And now I'm putting my energy where it's better suited.

Look at me, I can be healthy too.

Give the girl a medal.

"Can I get one of those, Mom?" Roxie asks, pointing at the screen and the piece of crap toy the kid in the video is pretending is awesome.

I lightly ruffle her hair then lean down and press a kiss to her forehead. "Nice try, boo-boo. But you've already got pedis and brunch."

"Aw man," she says.

But she's smiling, knowing that she's pushed me as far as she's able.

And for the first time since she came into my room a full thirty-six hours before, I breathe out a sigh of relief.

She's going to be okay.

———

I don't know the moment that I lost my battle with sleep, but I'm drawn back to consciousness by the sound of soft voices.

"...no," Stefan is saying, "don't wake her. I just need to step out to make a couple of phone calls and rearrange a few appointments."

Diane sighs and her tone is sharper than normal, cutting through the last of my sleep-hazed mind. "Does *Brit* know what those appointments are about?"

"Mom," he says on a sigh. "I've had enough of this conversation."

"Well, *I* haven't," she snaps. "If you filing for divorce from the woman you love wasn't enough then being in the hospital with your daughter who's recovering from surgery should be the reality check you need."

"*Mom.*"

"You need to tell her."

Tell me what?

I want to move, to pop my head up and demand he talk to me, fucking *talk* to me.

Finally.

But if I hold still, if I pretend to be asleep, maybe I'll find out the real reason he left me.

And I have the feeling *that's* far more important than inter-jecting myself into this conversation. Because I know Stefan's tone. It's locking into stubborn as fuck, the same kind of impene-trable stubborn I battled through numerous times in my relation-ship with him.

The same kind of stubborn he can never maintain in the face of his mom.

Because he and Diane have been through too much together.

Because he loves his mom with all the fierce protectiveness of a son looking after his mother.

Because...

He won't give with me.

But he can't withstand her.

However, in all my plotting, I don't take our daughter into account.

She shifts in the bed next to me, voice as groggy as I know mine would have been a couple of minutes ago. "Grandma?"

Stefan's voice—in the middle of telling Diane to drop it—cuts off and there's a long blip of silence before Diane speaks, leaning over the bed (presumably, considering I'm still faking being asleep, but the mattress shakes, the bed shifts slightly). "I'm here, honey," she whispers. "I've brought you a change of clothes and—"

Right.

I've had enough pretending.

Mostly because my back is killing me, but also because their conversation is moving to normal volume and continuing to fake unconsciousness is going to get ridiculous.

I sigh quietly, roll my shoulders and neck then slowly push up, blinking at Diane—who smiles at me, a smile that freezes, eyes sharpening when she studies me.

Also, *right*.

Likely not fooling her with my pretending.

"Hey," I say softly, getting to my feet with a wince and rounding the bed to pull her into a hug. "You didn't have to come by."

"Stefan mentioned Rox had spilled on her clothes"—the ones I'd carefully changed her into in anticipation of blowing this popsicle joint—"so I figured that I would bring some clean ones by."

Thankfully, Mr. Fluffernut had been spared the indignity of getting stained with strawberry Jell-O.

"That was nice of you," I tell her.

"Anything for my granddaughter." She leans in, kisses my cheek, murmurs for my ears only, "Anything for *you*." A quick squeeze and then she releases me, stepping back and clapping her hands together. "Now, Roxie girl, why don't I keep Mr. Fluffernut safe while you and Mom get changed into clean clothes?"

"Okay, Nana," Roxie says, passing over the stuffed cat.

I reach for Rox, but Stefan beats me to it, leaning in, scooping her up and carefully setting her on her feet. I take hold of her arm, making sure she doesn't fall, but the contact brings Stefan and my fingers into contact.

Sparks of sensation shooting up my arm.

He drops his hold like he's been burned, steps back.

And I...

Well, I don't know what the fuck is up with him, with his secrets, with whatever he's hiding that Diane is pushing him to tell me, but he won't...

But I meant what I thought earlier.

I'm done with this, done with the turmoil and hurt and feeling like I'm not good enough—or like I've made a grave mistake but can't begin to comprehend how to fix it.

And...I'm done with the guilt.

With taking full responsibility for having done wrong.

This isn't just me.

We didn't fall apart after more than a decade together solely because of my actions.

Stefan is responsible too.

That settles deep, settles heavy, but I just look down at Roxie and smile.

Focus on what's important.

"Let's get you changed."

Twenty-One

Stefan

"You're messing up the best thing that's ever happened to you."

A pulse of pain slices through my temple. "Mom, swear to God."

She lifts up on tiptoe, presses a kiss to my cheek. "I love you, but you're a mess, baby." Then, before I can respond and tell her —a-*fucking*-gain—to mind her own business, she pats my jaw, shoves Mr. Fluffernut into my arms. "I'm going down to meet your father. We'll see you back at Brit's house."

I nod. "Drive safe."

Her face softens, and she touches my cheek again, any trace of frustration leaving her eyes. "Always looking after me, my baby boy, aren't you?"

"Mom—"

"So, when are you going to trust the people who love you to look after you in turn?"

That settles like an anchor chained to my heart, pushed overboard and sent down into the darkening blue depths, drawing me further and further under the frigid water.

Or maybe that's the reality of the future I've been looking toward smacking me in the face.

Likely knowing she struck deep with that, she pats my cheek again. "Tell the girls I'll see them back at the house."

I nod woodenly, tongue stuck to the roof of my mouth.

And then she's gone.

And I'm left alone with my thoughts.

And my regrets.

———

"Can you move the pillow a little higher?" Rox asks Tiff.

Tiff—ever-patient as always—adjusts the pillow to Queen Roxie's liking. "That good?"

"Uh-huh."

A flick of her gaze over her shoulder, mouth curving, eyes dancing. Then Tiff is looking back to Roxie. "Okay little munchkin," she says, holding up the bottles of nail polish, "what color do you want?"

I leave them pondering the merits of fire engine red with gold sparkles over alternating sky blue and sunshine yellow.

Brit and my parents are in the kitchen, holding a quiet conversation, though I'm able to pick up enough of it to dive right in.

"I'll skip the games if I need to," Brit's saying, pointing to the screen on her cell. "But this is the team's schedule for the next couple of weeks. Dan"—her brother—"is going to come on Sunday and stay for a week or so. I think by then Rox will be good to go back to school and I'll focus on hiring a nanny to cover my time—"

I frown.

"—I should have done that a long time ago—"

I open my mouth, but she keeps going.

"—that was my mistake. I just..." She presses her lips flat, releases them. "Well, I'll make sure it's fixed and—"

My mom reaches out and takes her hand. "We love you both, honey. We're happy to help out in any way."

"That goes with this stuff," my dad says then nods at her phone. "And with the team. Family comes first."

A statement that flies through the air and sinks deep into my belly like a sharp as shit blade.

I grit my teeth, exhale silently. "I'll be here."

Three heads swivel in my direction.

"You don't need to hire a nanny," I say. "When you're with the team, I've got Roxie."

There's a long pause.

Then Brit clears her throat. "That's exactly what we were trying to avoid when we hammered out custody. You're not responsible for covering my time while I'm working." Her tone grows more than a little frosty, and I know I deserve it. "Especially when you were so unhappy doing that during our marriage—"

Another jab to the middle.

"You can stay here as long as you want, of course. I won't take that away from Rox. But I'll make sure there's a responsible adult covering me when I'm not here."

I could point out that *I* am a responsible adult.

But that would just work at undoing all of the shit I had been trying to work toward since I asked for the divorce.

So, I just nod, lift one shoulder in a shrug, and say, "If that's what you want."

I'm looking for a sign—I can't pretend I'm not—that she's lying, that she wants me to argue and demand a presence in her life.

I've seen that fight, that hope over and over these last months.

It's not here today though.

It's replaced with determination that has my insides twisting, that lance in my belly sinking deeper, twisting for good measure.

I know that determination.

It's what got her into the NHL, has helped her stay there.

It's unstoppable.

And it means...that I've officially lost her.

It's what I wanted these last months, what I needed.

So...

Why does it feel like my world has just ended?

A couple of hours of waiting on Queen Rox (and giving the proper amount of appreciation for her manicure—Caribbean Blue and fittingly, Emperor Purple), my parents take off.

We've all eaten. Rested. Watched lots and lots of YouTube videos.

Tiff braided her hair.

My mom read her book after book.

My dad talked her through the financial viability of being an influencer.

Brit got her pillows and blankets situated just right before taking off for the rink.

Now, though, Queen Rox has settled into the deep sleep of a kiddo who's recovering from surgery.

I'll poke my head in later, but I know that she's officially down for the count.

And...the Gold game is on in a few minutes.

I flick off the light, walk out into the hall, and head downstairs. The kitchen lights are on, but the room is empty—even though the delicious smell of something spicy and savory hangs in the air. The soft rumble of the TV draws me to the family room and I see that Tiff has left a plate on the coffee table for me, along with a can of beer.

My heart warms at the sight, knowing this is Tiff's way of caring—cooking more food, ensuring Brit and I make up for the missed meals at the hospital, doing something to keep busy when times are tense.

She looks up when I come into the room, eyes shifting away

from the TV and the pregame programming for the Gold. "I figured you'd want to watch."

Because I always watch—a fucking glutton for punishment.

She clears her throat. "I'll, uh, take off once I finish eating and cleaning up—"

"You don't have to go," I tell her softly.

She freezes with her own can of beer halfway to her mouth. "Yeah," she says softly. "I really do. Brit—"

"Isn't part of this conversation." I sit down on the couch and pull the plate toward me.

Tiff snorts. "This is her house."

"Yes," I mutter, "and she told you to stay as long as you want."

"I think I've already overstayed my welcome."

"Brit isn't like that," I remind her. "She knows that you and Roxie are important to each other."

Tiff sighs and looks away, but doesn't engage further, just finishes her dinner and her beer, takes my empty plate from me when I finish.

"You don't have—"

She waves me off and turns for the kitchen. A minute later, I'm listening to the sounds of the water running, to the dishwasher being loaded.

Then the water cutting off.

The door to the dishwasher closing.

I get up before she can scoot out the front door without saying goodbye, catching her in the hall, purse in hand, guilty look on her face.

What's with my life being full of difficult women?

A thought I obviously keep in my own head as I take her coat from the rack, hold it up for her to slip her arms into.

But I don't let her walk away when it's on.

Instead, I draw her back against me, hug her tightly. "You are not what your mom says you are."

She shudders but doesn't fight my hold. "I'm not so sure

about that," she whispers. "I mean, look at what I'm doing with my life."

"Going to school? Working?"

"And leaving her to—" She exhales, shakes her head, pushes at my arm around her middle.

I release her. "To what?" I ask softly. "Figure her own life out after you spent too much of yours living for her?"

Tiff glances away, muscle in her jaw ticking, eyes slammed shut. "Yeah."

"Do you see how fucked up that is?"

Those lids flash open. "I'm not the only one with a fucked-up situation," she says, brows lifting pointedly as she glances around the space.

"You know what's going down with Brit and I."

"*I* know," she says. "But Brit doesn't." She tilts her head to the side, pinning me in place with brown eyes that are nothing like the chocolate of my wife's. "And are you planning on *letting* her know?"

"Tiff," I warn.

"Because any idiot can see that she's still in love with you."

Fucking. Stubborn. Ass. Women.

"That's not—"

"The truth?" She shakes her head, ponytail flying behind her. "You're delusional if you don't think she would get back with you in a second."

That lance strikes home again, piercingly painful. Probably because that *has* been the truth of it, what my inner asshole is clinging onto—that I can fix it. When it's all over, I can fix it and make everything right with Brit.

But that's also not what I saw on Brit's face in the kitchen.

Determination. Stubbornness.

To move on from me.

And *that* has my stomach churning.

I scowl. "That's not what we're discussing—"

"You're right," she says. "We weren't." A lift of one brow. "*Now* we are."

Again. Fucking. Stubborn. Ass. Women.

"I'm watching the game," I mutter, spinning toward the family room.

"We weren't discussing it," she says, ignoring me and taking my hand, squeezing firmly. "But I think, at some point, you're going to have to talk about it with someone."

How the fuck we went from me comforting her about her shitshow of a mother to her chastising me about Brit and well... other shit, I don't know.

But I *do* know that I'm fucking tired of it all.

"Game's on," I say, pulling free.

"Stefan—"

I give her my back, start for the family room, for the TV and my ex-wife taking up the screen during a pregame interview.

More jabs.

More regrets.

More knowing that they don't make one bit of difference.

"Stay and watch it with me," I say icily. "Or just go home, yeah?"

Twenty-Two

BRIT

I left my husband with his girlfriend in my kitchen.

Yup, even *I* know how fucked up that particular scene was.

But I set it aside, breathe against the vise-like grip that thought threatens to have over my insides, and focus on the one thing I *can* control at the moment.

My warm-up.

I'm starting—thank fuck—because sitting on the bench watching the game develop around me, the guys all part of it and me on the sidelines doing shit all?

Equally as much torture as that scene in the kitchen when I left.

Tiffany is great.

And I want to hate her.

Unfortunately for my heart and soul and the state of Roxie's freshly manicured nails, I can't.

"Brit—"

I look up from the bike, see that my teammate Josh is standing a couple of feet away. He's holding a protein shake—my preferred one because he's the captain and knows these things, but also because he's a good guy who likes to take care of the people he loves (case in point, helping his sister out of a bad relationship...and then not killing Ben, our teammate, when he fell for her).

He's that good guy and the captain, and I know it's both of them checking the pulse of my emotions as I slow my legs, draw the exercise bike to a halt, and hold my hand out for the shake.

"Thanks," I tell him, unscrewing the cap and taking a long glug of it.

His gaze holds mine. "Rox is good?"

"Healing faster than you or I would be, that's for sure."

He leans against the handlebars, deep brown eyes studying mine. "I don't think anything can stop a Plantain girl, that's for sure."

"She's a Barie," I say softly.

"No"—he nudges my foot with his own—"she's both." His mouth turns up. "Which is why I know that Brit fucking Plantain is going to kick ass for us tonight."

This man.

This team.

This family I'm lucky enough to be part of.

I finish off the shake, screw the cap back on. "Damn right, I am."

He snags the empty bottle, holds it up for me, lips still curved. But then his face grows serious, and he nudges my foot again. "But—"

I brace.

"—you're going to get some sleep right afterward, yeah?"

It's phrased as a question.

But it's definitely not one.

An order plain and simple.

It's tempting to tell him to fuck off, that I can manage my own life. But that's not how this team, this family works. "It's first on my agenda, Cap," I murmur.

He nods, claps a hand down onto my shoulder. "Good," he says. "And just so you know, I expect a shutout tonight."

I snort. "You know you just fucking cursed it, yeah?"

Because to have a shutout, you don't talk about shutouts.

"I don't believe in fate." He tosses the bottle into the recycle bin. "I believe in skill." A smirk as he takes off for the dressing room. "And I believe in your skill in particular, Banana-rama."

I roll my eyes.

That goddamned nickname.

But I don't fight it.

Because I have a fucking game to get ready for.

Despite Josh's faux pas of mentioning a shutout and likely jinxing it, we're well on the way to shutting down the Grizzlies' offense through all three periods.

Just a little more than two minutes left now, and the face-off is in the offensive zone, meaning that I'm watching my teammates' asses and trying to predict who's going to win the draw—

And if it's going to come my way in an odd man rush, or if they'll keep it on the opposite end of the ice for the rest of the game.

I wish I could say I wouldn't mind the former, that I'm bored and ready for some action.

But...

I'm tired.

I want the game to be over, and I want to go home.

The whistle *trills* and I crouch, getting ready for the drop, which happens a bare heartbeat later, the centers' sticks coming together in a *crack* of sound. I watch the puck deflect off the ref's skates and bounce into the corner, our winger hustling forward but not getting there in time to make that first touch.

The puck rings around the boards, and is kept in by Josh, who shoots it over to our other defenseman. He's young and new to the roster, and when he faces the quick burst of pressure from the Grizzlies, he panics—easy to see even from the other side of the ice—flicking the biscuit towards the net with a quick wrist shot.

Unfortunately those types of panic-driven tosses of the puck very rarely get through.

These guys are too good at crowding the middle and blocking shots and protecting their goalies to let a squeaker get through on the regular.

Not to say that it *doesn't* happen—there are always fuck-ups, bounces go the wrong way, and the hockey gods are cruel.

But the panicked shot when we're up two to zero with—my eyes flick to the clock—now just over a minute to go, are fucking killing me.

Because that's not smart hockey.

Because I know where this is going.

The puck hits one of our opponents' shin guards with a resounding *thud*.

And it bounces hard.

Out of reach of my guys.

Over the blue line.

Out of the offensive zone.

They're good, though—my team and the Grizzlies. They react quickly, are on the puck in an instant, battling for it in the neutral zone—the middle of the ice, the space between the blue lines—fighting it out in an effort to regain control.

Josh skates hard for the puck, picking it up, trying to make a pass. It connects, but not cleanly, bouncing over Lucas's stick blade, sending him off-balance as he struggles to corral it. The fumble takes a bare half of second, but it's enough for the Grizzlies to close ranks, two on him as they wrestle the puck away.

And now they're carrying it into our zone.

Into my fucking domain, moving with speed toward my net.

Josh is chasing. His D partner is way the fuck out of the play. Lucas is back-checking hard along with the rest of the forwards.

Two on one.

Not the worst.

It could be two on none, me by myself, trying not to fuck shit up.

I take one hard cut, moving myself to the top of the crease, cutting the angle, but playing conservatively because they're coming fast and there's not a lot of time left, and then I'm watching, waiting them out, playing hockey's version of chicken.

I know these guys.

Know these two.

Know the passes they like to make, what their bodies look like when they wind up for a shot.

And I know that Josh is going to be back in time to cover one of them, that Lucas and the others are going to put pressure on the other, going to prevent the Grizzlies' teammates from joining in.

So, I know that it's going to be me and...Gray Roberts, one of the top forwards of the Grizzlies. A leftie with a preference for right wing, but with a wicked shot that can strike from anywhere.

This kid—because, God, the former number one draft pick is a fucking *baby*—has been taking the league by storm, racking up points left and right.

Particularly with unexpected shots that he releases with his weight on his back foot (something that's hard as hell to do, and something I don't see all that often).

But it's something—along with the other facts—that ricochets through my brain in an instant.

I'm still tracking the puck, still watching, still moving.

But that information is flying through my mind and I'm making adjustments, lasering in on what I need to be focused on.

That weight shift.

The way he draws back the puck.

The fake pass.

And the shot that comes flying toward an open part of my goal.

Open because I left it that way.

Because I know I can cover it and I *want* him to shoot there.

And because I think I can get the rookie to bite.

And...

He does.

But that shot is so fucking wicked, so goddamned fast that he still almost scores anyway.

I dig in my skates, push past my fatigue, the pain in my side, and...

I *move.*

Or flop like an ungraceful fish, anyway.

But I manage to get a piece of the puck, deflecting it behind the net, scrambling up to my skates—still ungracefully—as I search for the puck, see it bouncing toward the boards.

Then Josh is there, scooping it up, the Grizzlies on him hard.

I risk a look in front of me, clock where the players are, and then look back in time to see that little fucker, Gray, snag the puck from him, flinging it back toward me.

It comes high and precisely at neck level, and I stand up straighter so that it doesn't throat chop me, wincing when it clips my collarbone, something that still hurts, even with my pads.

Then I'm shaking that off, dropping back down as it heads for the ice, trying to beat it there, or meet it there, or, hell, to just fucking cover it so we can get a whistle and reset.

I hit the crease, stretch an arm out and...

I'm bumped, sending the puck squirting out to the side, sending me back to my ungraceful fishy thrashing again.

Sticking my leg out and blocking the shot they try to tap in.

Jumping forward, corralling the puck under my glove, only to get a stick to my hand for my trouble.

The puck slips out...

Slides right over to Gray.

And from my full-on beached-whale position on my back on the ice, I know I'm...fucked.

He winds up—

The buzzer sounds.

Whistles blow.

The game's over.

Gray lifts his stick, leaves the puck where it is, barely two feet in front of the net, and winks at me, mouthing, "Next time," before skating away, heading over to his team's bench.

Cocky little shit.

I collapse back onto the ice but can't help smiling.

Kid's got talent and attitude and balls, I have to give him that.

"Told you you'd kick ass," Josh says, nudging me with his stick.

I groan, clamber up to my feet, turning to accept the post-game hugs and fist-bumps from my teammates, but I'm still grumbling at Josh.

"You had to talk about shutouts, didn't you?"

He winks, and it's the grown-up version of Gray's. "Did you, or did you not accomplish that?"

I roll my eyes, smack his shoulder.

But he's not wrong.

And I know I'm smiling the entire way to the locker room.

TWENTY-THREE

STEFAN

I didn't hear her come in from the game, didn't hear her retrieve her post-game snack or watch whatever tape the video coaches pulled for her as she eats her veggies and hummus and drinks her chocolate milk.

But I do hear her soft footsteps down the hall, nearly silent as she passes the door to the guest suite.

Similarly quiet as she climbs the stairs, only the squeaky fourth riser giving her away.

A pause, the whole house seeming to draw in a breath and hold it.

Then she continues to climb.

I don't know why I get out of bed.

I shouldn't.

But...I watched her in the game (without Tiff, who wisely left my grumpy ass to complete that activity by myself), and I watched her fight for the win, then for the shutout, and...

I remembered the way I saw the fight leave her eyes in the kitchen earlier.

So...some part of me *can't* keep from throwing back the

covers, sliding out of bed, moving up the stairs—and skipping the fourth, squeaky one.

I can't stop myself from walking down the hall, from listening outside Roxie's room as Brit checks on her.

I can't stop myself from slipping into her room, and waiting, seeing the bedside lamp on, her snack positioned on the wooden surface, the iPad loaded and video to review ready on the mattress, its bright glare obvious in the otherwise dim space.

A soft *thud* of a door being quietly shut.

More footsteps.

And then—

"Jesus fucking Christ, Stefan," she snaps, skittering to a stop, her hand clamped over her chest. "What the hell are you doing?"

I don't know *what* I'm doing.

Or maybe I do.

Maybe I've decided that I need to *un*do everything.

Maybe I'm just a fucking dumbass.

I barely resist the urge to shove my hands into my hair, to clench the locks, to turn around and escape from the room.

But I *do* resist, and when I get a good look at Brit, at her face, her eyes, the pain written into the lines of her expression and the dark circles beneath her lower lashes...

I come up with the reason I'm in her room.

Why I'm pushing myself into her life when I was so determined to keep myself out of it.

Because she's exhausted and in pain and she needs some fucking rest.

"Brit," I say, moving toward her. "You need to go to bed."

She lifts a brow, looks around the space deliberately—and yeah, I know I'm making that a little difficult right now, considering I've invaded her bedroom.

But that's not what I mean.

She needs to have that snack and go to sleep.

She needs to give her body the proper time to rest.

She needs to watch video in the morning and not stay up for hours tonight.

I open my mouth to tell her all of that, but I don't get the chance to because—

I'm too busy being an idiot.

I march by her, snag the tablet, and power it off. "Fine," I snap, tucking it under my arm. "I'll just keep this until morning." A beat. "*After* you've had a full night's sleep."

Because she needs that and hasn't gotten it, and—

"Don't you fucking dare," she growls, reaching for the iPad.

I hold it up out of range. "Sleep. You can have it in the morning."

"I'm not a goddamned child," she grinds out.

"You're certainly acting like it."

"So says the man who's pushed his way into my room and is trying to control what I do. You gave up on having any say in that when you asked for a divorce." She sniffs. "And anyway, I can take care of myself."

"Yeah?" I droll out, rage boiling beneath my skin. "Is that really the angle you want to go with?"

"Just give me the iPad." She grabs at it. "Even someone as stubborn as you has got to see the irony of you keeping me up when if this conversation was just *over*"—she grunts as I lift the tablet higher—"I could go to sleep sooner."

"You want to talk about stubborn?" I snap. "Really?"

She narrows her eyes at me.

"Have you forgotten that you were fucking *shot*," I snap. "And you didn't miss a fucking game."

Fury flashes through chocolate-brown depths. "First, it was a fucking graze, and you know it. I had two stitches. Two! Meanwhile, Lucas almost died, and the kids—" She breaks off on a shudder. "*They* almost—" Another. "I went to the doctor. I got it checked out and stitched up. There was nothing to worry about."

"Oh?" I ask dryly. "Is that why you hid it from Mandy?"

She winces. "Mandy and everyone had enough to worry about."

"And that's why it's *still* bothering you?" I flick my brows up. "Why it even bothered you in the game tonight and Mandy thinks you injured a rib instead of the truth?"

"That's not relevant to this conversation—"

"You haven't been the same since that day in the field at The Dairy, you *know* you haven't."

"Of course I haven't been the same!" She tosses up her hands but at least gives up on the iPad for the moment. "No one from the team has been the same. A fucking madman opened fire and targeted innocent people and kids and we almost *lost* someone we love. It's impossible to remain unchanged in that."

She has a point, but I can't bring myself to acknowledge it.

She's still talking anyway. "Bad shit happens, but we're supposed to find a way for it to bring us together, to draw us closer—"

"Yet you didn't let it stop you from getting right back on the ice, did you?" I snap. "Didn't give a shit about almost losing loved ones and life being put into perspective when you went right back out there and away from us."

She presses her lips flat for one long moment. "That's not fair."

"Isn't it?"

"You promised you'd never stand between me and hockey."

My heart squeezes.

Because I absolutely promised that.

"Did I stop you from playing?" A beat. "Even then?"

She exhales, shakes her head, and I know she's trying to keep her voice calm when she says, "Did I go back too soon? Yeah, I did. I thought the team needed me, and—"

"The *team* needed you? Not Rox and I?"

That's a low blow, I know, after she worked so fucking hard to bring the team together, to create that family she'd always longed for.

The family *I* love too.

The family I absolutely consider my own as well.

It's just—

"That's not fair," she whispers. "And you know it."

I inhale sharply, hold it long enough to feel my lungs protest, but it still doesn't help me control my emotions, doesn't refocus me away from this shit storm of a conversation back onto what I should be concentrating on—

Getting Brit to rest.

Because she needs it, and I love her enough to make sure she gets it.

Fuck.

I can't think *that* shit.

She clenches her jaw tightly, eyes sliding from mine, clearly taking my silence personally.

Then she looks back and I see she's chosen violence.

I brace, but I don't do it fast enough or strongly enough to withstand the force of her question.

"Why did you *really* divorce me, Stefan?" she asks quietly.

I wince, stagger back a step.

"Because I know that it's not about me being shot."

Another step away from her.

She follows me. "And I know it's not about hockey or my traveling or even you disagreeing with my coming out of retirement."

One more step back and I find myself bumping into the wall.

"It's not about wanting more kids—" she begins.

I clench my teeth together so tightly that a bolt of pain shoots through my jaw.

"So why, really?" she presses. "Why did you sit downstairs and ask for a divorce? Why did you spend months pushing me away? What secret are you keeping from me?"

I don't have a choice.

Really, I don't.

Or maybe it's that I'm willing to do *anything*, absolutely

anything, to avoid having this conversation.

Maybe that's why I do it.

Why I drop the iPad onto the dresser. Why I snag her arm and draw her flush against me.

And maybe it's why I drop my mouth to hers and kiss her with every bit of emotion that's in my heart, my soul—frustration and longing, anger and need, fear and love, yes fucking *love.* I take advantage of her gasp of surprise—or maybe outrage—to slip my tongue into her mouth, to taste her as deeply as I can.

I feel her gorgeous body start to melt against mine, but then she suddenly goes stiff, suddenly shoves hard at my chest. "What the fuck, Stefan?" she snaps when our mouths come apart.

A fair question.

It's only that her next words throw me.

"You have a fucking girlfriend," she growls. "Jesus Christ. What's the matter with you?"

"I—" I shake my head. "A what?"

"A fucking—"

"Mom!"

Her eyes go wide at the sound of Roxie's voice, and she drops her arms, steps away from me, already moving for the hall.

"Stop," I say, snagging her arm. "I've got her," I say. "You should get in bed."

She grabs my thumb and bends it back so quickly that I barely track the movement, and then all I'm doing is tracking the pain, the intense need to relieve the pressure shooting up my arm.

Before I can find a way to make that happen, she releases me, getting in my face. "You've done a lot to me over the years, Stefan Barie"—she jabs a finger into my chest—"and I know I'm not innocent either but, I swear to God, if you stand between me and my daughter, I will fucking *end* you."

And then she's gone, a flash of blond disappearing from my periphery.

And leaving me rocked to the very core.

Then again, that's her superpower, isn't it?

Twenty-Four

BRIT

I know that he's waiting for me.

I just...hope that he isn't.

So, I take plenty of time to settle my little girl, take plenty of time to tuck her in and refill her water glass and make sure that she's not in any pain.

Which she's not, crazy kid of mine.

Recovering from surgery in no time, and I'm still feeling ouch over a couple of stitches and a strained muscle all these months later.

I shake my head to myself, continue reading the chapter even though she's fully out and I'll have to reread it tomorrow.

Buying time.

Delaying.

Pointless.

How about trying to get my lips to stop tingling and my pussy to stop being a needy fucking bitch?

Oh, and my heart to stop being so damned—

Heart like.

I sigh, quietly close the book, and set it to the side, knowing that I'm just delaying the inevitable. Still, I take the time to tuck in Mr. Fluffernut beside her, straighten the blankets, press one last kiss to my precious girl's forehead before slipping back out into the hall, closing the door behind me.

And yup, he's right there.

Right *fucking* there.

Sighing, I start to move by him but he doesn't let me, taking my arm in a firm grip.

I don't fight him—not there in the hall where we might wake Rox—just allow him to draw me into my bedroom, to close the door behind him.

"Let me go," I growl.

"No," he snaps. "No fucking way." He turns us, pins me back against the wall. "What the fuck did you say?"

"About why you divorced me? About the secret you're clearly hiding?"

His expression is stark, but his eyes burn with fury. "No, baby." He drops his head, locks our gazes together. "About me having a girlfriend."

My brows snap together and I feel outrage. "Tiffany is a nice woman and she deserves better." I lift my chin. "As you well know."

"Tiff *is* a nice woman, but"—his eyes flash—"baby, when have I ever said that Tiff was my girlfriend?"

"She's—" I break off, doubt creeping into my heart.

"When?" he presses.

I blink.

"*When?*"

I finally manage to stumble out, "I-I've seen her over at your place for dinner with your parents. She took Roxie for mani-pedis, picked her up from school, from practice."

"And?"

"And," I whisper, throat tight. "I saw you two all over each other on your porch."

"I know." He steps closer, the front of his body pressing,

thighs to chest, to mine. "But. When. Have. I. Ever. Said. Tiff. Is. My. Girlfriend?"

I freeze then, the hope I'd set aside blooming unbidden inside me. "What?"

His hand lifts and I can't help it.

I flinch.

Remembering all the hurts, all the times the tender feelings in my belly were crushed beneath the heel of his boot.

He hesitates, palm just inches from my skin, and then he's touching me.

Lightly, softly, the barest stroke of his fingers over my jaw. "She's not my girlfriend, baby," he murmurs and that hope grows further, until it's pressing all along the inside of my torso, my rib cage. "She never has been, never will be." He shifts, drawing nearer, cupping my cheek, tilting my face up so all I see is him.

Not Stefan Barie, cold and untouchable.

But Stefan Barie, the husband I knew. The man who loves every single part of me, warts and all. The person who became my safe space.

Who is the other half of my soul.

It's...too much.

Those feelings. The love in my heart. The pain of knowing it's going to go away again.

"No," I whisper.

"There will *never* be another woman," he says softly, as though his words aren't shredding right through my insides.

My eyes are burning with tears, desperation and hope clinging to my soul.

Then why put us through this? Fucking *why?*

I open my mouth to ask, but then he's cupping both of my cheeks, and...

He's kissing me.

Deep and long and...I don't have the strength to stop him, not with what he told me, not with how gentle his hands are on my face, and how good his body feels against mine.

I *can't* stop him.

Not when he threads an arm behind me, scooping me up, encouraging me to wrap my legs around him.

Not when he carries me to the bed, still kissing me.

Not when he comes down over the top of me, hands in my hair, knocking my ponytail askew, lips sliding from mine along my jaw, and to my ear, to that sensitive spot just behind it.

"Never anyone but you."

I love hearing that.

And I hate it.

Because why the fuck did we go through all of this only to get right back here?

And...can I do this? Can I come back? Can I move on from all that happened?

I'm not sure that's possible.

But I'm also not sure that I can stop myself from trying.

"Me, baby," he says, nipping at my earlobe. "Stop thinking so hard and focus on me."

"I don't know if I can," I whisper.

"Then focus on the way I make you feel," he says against the skin of my throat. "Think about how you feel when I kiss your breasts and suck on your nipples. Think about how much you like it when I kiss along your stomach, when I part your legs and bury my face in that wet pussy of yours."

I spread my legs, wanting that very much.

Something he notices because his mouth curves. "You want that, baby? Want my tongue inside you? My fingers fucking you?"

"I want that." No hesitation.

Because my vagina is a little hussy, and it's way ahead of every protective instinct in my mind and heart telling me to stop, to slow down, to think this through.

If there's anything I've learned, it's that the future is not set in stone.

So, I don't take the words back, but I also don't lay there like a pillow princess. If I'm going down this path, potentially making this idiotic mistake, then the least I can do is be a full and active participant. I sit up, nudging him back from me, tugging my sweatshirt and tee off in one smooth movement. I'm left in my sports bra, but before he can reach for that, I'm grabbing his T-shirt, yanking it over his head, tossing it to the side to join the pile of my clothes.

God, I love his chest.

It's strong and broad with the barest dusting of hair. Paired with his beard and it's like fucking a Viking.

My Viking.

Which is dangerous thinking, but I don't get the chance to get caught up in it, not when he's reaching for the band of my sports bra and stretching it enough to pull it off—

Or pull it *up*.

Stopping the moment my boobs pop free, leaving the band bunched beneath my arms.

But I don't care.

Not when he's cupping my breasts, massaging my flesh, rolling the hard buds of my nipples between thumbs and fore-fingers.

"God," I whisper, dropping my head back. "That's good."

"Mmm," he murmurs, head dropping, lips sealing around one taut nipple, sucking deeply.

"Oh!" I gasp, fingers tightening in his hair, holding him to me.

And he stays, sucking the sensitive bud deeply into his mouth, and doing it for long enough to make my head spin, for sweat to gather behind my knees, in the crooks of my arms, for moisture to slicken my pussy, making it ache in emptiness.

That persistent pang has me reaching for him, slipping my hand into the waistband of his sweats, and—

"Oh," I whisper as I wrap my hand around the hard length of him. "God, I've missed this."

A chuckle around my nipple that has me shivering, has my hand tensing.

And him groaning.

I flex my fingers again. "I want you in my mouth, baby."

Teeth in my flesh, a groan against my skin, and I know he's warning me to behave, to lie back and let him pleasure me.

But...I've done enough lying back, enough waiting around.

I stroke him hard once, twice, enough to get him off-balance, to distract him from my breasts...

And then I pounce.

TWENTY-FIVE

STEFAN

One second, I'm tasting her.

The next, I'm losing my mind.

Her tits bounce as she pushes me back, sending me toppling to the mattress as she clambers on top of me.

Then she's gripping the edge of her bra, yanking it up and over her head, tossing it to the side.

All the right parts jiggle and I'm focused on that, so focused on her pinkened skin, the hard buds of her nipples, the urge to cup her breasts in my hands again that when she reaches for the waistband of my sweats and starts to yank them down, I don't immediately fight her.

Just lift my hips and help her shove them out of the way, all the better to get my dick free.

And then it's popping out, springing toward her hands like it's begging for her touch, for her mouth.

And, hell, who the fuck am I kidding?

It *is* begging for her touch, for the slickness of her mouth, for—

"Oh God," I groan, fisting the bedspread, trying to resist the urge to grab her head and force her to take my cock into her mouth.

She laughs softly but doesn't make me beg.

Just parts her lips and sucks me deep.

Sensation explodes over me—wet and hot, tight and rough, her tongue flicking out to tease the head of my dick, making me shiver and groan, desperate for—

"Fuck!"

Teeth.

For her dragging her teeth lightly up my shaft, taking me deep enough that I bump against the back of her throat.

She laughs softly, but even as I'm processing that sound, as I'm reveling in the beauty of that feminine confidence, she's taken over, she's showing me no mercy, putting every bit of knowledge she's gained of me over the last decade plus to devastating use.

And it's dangerous.

Because, just like that, I'm seconds away from coming down her throat.

I haven't been with anyone.

I've barely used my hand.

Fuck, I pretty much thought that my dick didn't work any longer.

But I should have known better—ever since I fell in love with Brit, I've only wanted one woman.

And now I'm in the presence of her again, now I've got a chance to put this bullshit behind us and...

Go back?

No.

But maybe I can hold off long enough that I can fix it...

Can finish it.

And then come back to her.

Maybe...maybe I can do that.

Maybe I *have* to do that.

She hums as she takes me deep again, grip so tight that I'm

seeing stars, strokes so damned good, so much fucking better than my own hand that my orgasm coils tightly at the base of my spine.

One more second and I'm going to explode.

I grip her beneath her armpits, tugging her off my dick with a sharp *pop* of sound.

I miss the heat and wet and pressure of her tongue and teeth and lips.

But I need to taste her more.

I shove her back, and she bounces against the mattress, blond hair spreading out on her pillow, smile small but sexy as hell.

And then she's reaching for her sweats, shoving them and her underwear down, leaving me with a glorious view of that sopping pussy of hers, spreading her legs and letting me see the folds glistening in the overhead lights.

I need to taste her.

Right now.

So, I do, shoving her legs further apart with my shoulders, dropping down, burying my face into her cunt, stroking my tongue through her labia, up to her clit, tasting the sweet tang of her desire, knowing it's coating my face, my beard, dripping off my chin.

Knowing and fucking *loving* it.

I suck hard at her clit, slide a finger into the tight sheath of her pussy, feel it clamp around me, know that she's as on edge as I am.

That we can make ourselves come, self-love to oblivion.

But it's never like *this*.

The spark, the sense of rightness, of our hearts and souls so perfectly complete that every sensation is multiplied a thousand-fold, that the pleasure I get from touching her, from making her cry out my name, from feeling her body shudder and jolt against mine is a hundred times better than any orgasm I could give myself.

I press the flat of my tongue against her clit, slide another finger into the tight sheath of her, knowing that I'm going to make her come this way, and then I'm going to coax her on top of me, get her to sit on my face and—

She gasps, head pressing back into the pillows, pussy clamping around me. "Stefan!"

"Come for me, baby."

"I—" Her hips undulate, and I know what she needs without having to think about it.

Another finger.

A firmer press of my tongue.

"Stef— Fuck—" Her hips buck. Her head presses down harder into the pillow. "I—"

Teeth against her clit.

"Oh God!"

Her pussy clamps hard.

Her thighs tighten around my shoulders.

And she's coming apart.

Pleased, I groan against her cunt, lapping up the evidence of her desire, feeling her body shiver and convulse around me.

"Again," I growl, nipping at her thigh, sending her jolting.

"What?" she asks blearily, eyes going wide. "Stefan, I—"

But I'm already moving, flipping to my back and taking her with me, rolling her, shifting her up—

So that pussy is an inch in front of my face.

"Honey," she murmurs. "I'm too—"

I grab that lush ass of hers and yank her down, nearly smothering myself in the process. But what a fucking way to go, drowning in her desire, her pleasure, her need, surrounded on all sides by her.

She groans, hips bucking, alternating between grinding against my lips, my beard, my teeth and tongue and trying to lift up.

Not too sensitive, I can see that in her eyes.

She loves this.

It's driving her right back up to the edge.

So, instead, she's worried about asphyxiating me.

And I want her coming, not worried about whether or not I'm going to die—

A thought that has me freezing, has me still, has me out of this moment.

Something Brit notices.

Fuck.

I'm nose-deep in her pussy and worry is eating at my erection, my orgasm suddenly a thousand miles away.

"Honey—"

I shudder.

For too long she didn't call me that.

I'm not going to fuck it up now.

I grasp that ass, tug her down onto me again, rebury my face in her pussy, and I focus on doing everything I can to make her come.

She gasps, hips bucking, grinding against me as I delve my tongue into her, as I taste and stroke and—

"Stefan," she groans, more of her weight dropping onto me, her hands grasping the headboard, banging it against the wall as her hips start moving, as she grinds against me, as—

I make her come again.

Fucking perfect.

Fucking beautiful.

Her back arches, tits bouncing, cheeks flushed, eyes slammed closed.

And all the while that pussy clamps around my fingers, her orgasm turning her body into a tight ball of muscle...and then a limp pile of woman, slumping to the side.

I guide her off me, settling her head onto the pillows, her eyes barely open. "Don't think this gets you out of talking to me," she slurs.

I grin, lighter than I've been in more than a year.

Lighter than I've been since I found out—

I hold back a grimace, cut the thoughts off.

Maybe I should let her go to sleep—she certainly is just a

couple of minutes away from that right now. I should gather her close, tuck her against me, and allow us both to just...sleep.

But...

What if I don't get another chance at this?

What if I wake up and she realizes this is the biggest mistake of her life?

I...

I need to seize this opportunity.

I need to *live*.

I start to move over her, but her lids are closed and—

Fuck.

Dick hard or not, having this potentially last chance or not...I can't do this. Not when she's exhausted. Not when she's been through too much.

"Don't play the staid and moral hero now," she murmurs, lips curving, eyes staying closed, hand lifting, pushing lightly at my chest.

I laugh quietly, remembering another time when she said that, another lifetime.

But I don't move.

Which, I know, is why she pushes hard enough at my chest to roll me to my back.

Which, I know, is why she clambers on top of me, ungraceful for a change, but grace doesn't matter one fucking bit when she's grabbing my cock and lifting her hips, and—

Thank you, hockey gods.

She slides my dick right inside that tight wet heat.

Her rhythm is slow and lazy and I'm on such a hair trigger that I want to grip her hips, coax her to go faster, to flip her to her back, thrust hard and fast and deep like a rutting animal.

But...

I stay there with her on top of me, the lazy and unhurried grinding killing me, but knowing it's making her feel good, and that's enough.

I can withstand any amount of torture for her.

Even leaving her.

Even hurting her.

A bolt of shame cuts through me and I almost push her off, almost run right the fuck out of this room.

But then she leans down, one of her palms resting on my chest, her other coming to my cheek. "It's only ever been you, Stefan," she murmurs.

And I find I can't lie back, can't be patient.

Not when those words sew themselves into my soul.

I buck up and reverse our positions, start pounding into her.

And...

She takes it. She loves it. Wrapping her legs around me in turn, meeting me thrust for thrust.

Clamping tight.

Coming apart, my name on her lips.

And...I stop thinking—or stop thinking of anything other than the feel of her pussy fluttering, the sound of her moans, the way her body feels beneath me.

And I let myself fall.

TWENTY-SIX

BRIT

I should be sleeping.

I'm exhausted and pleasured and haven't had nearly enough sleep the last few nights.

But instead, I'm lying here, my mind twisting.

Because...

I'm waiting for him to leave.

Again.

Waiting for this moment to be over, for the words to not mean anything, for him to find a reason...

To go.

To retreat.

To leave me to my empty bed and my half-broken soul.

He sighs, his hand sliding forward, wrapping around my belly, drawing me against his heavy frame. "I did a number on you, didn't I?"

I cringe inwardly. "Stef—"

"I'll make it better," he says. "I'll make it up to you."

Make up for *what* exactly? Breaking my heart? Divorcing me?

Putting us all through this shit only to force his way back into my life, my home, my heart?

Fucking *why?*

But I don't get to make sense of it, I don't get a chance to ask those questions—

Or maybe I'm too chicken shit.

Because when he draws me more securely back against him, when he wraps that arm tightly around my middle, I...settle.

The sleep that's been clinging to the outer edges of my periphery crowds in. The exhaustion that's been drawing on my every cell since I came home from the game a few nights ago takes over.

I fall asleep.

And I do it hard.

———

I wake having absolutely no idea what time it is, just feeling like I've slept for a hundred fucking years.

I'm stiff as shit—my body feels as though I've been ridden hard and put up wet.

Very wet, considering the orgasms Stefan gave me.

But I'm alone in bed now, and I can't lie, my heart hurts a bit at that.

Sighing, I roll over, alternating between relief and wondering what in the fuck I'm doing—allowing my ex-husband to fuck me senseless while admitting to him that I've never loved another.

And doing it all without answers...and without a man in my arms when I wake up.

"It's one in the afternoon," I mutter, snagging my cell, seeing the time on the screen. "Of course he's not going to be here."

What's he going to do?

Lie next to me and watch me sleep?

I love the man, but that's too much closeness, even after all this time together. And apart.

And *together*.

Because I'm going to find him, and I'm going to tie him up if I have to, and...

I'm going to demand some fucking answers.

Good. Plan. Break.

I stifle a groan, toss back the blankets, and stand.

"Damn," I mutter, sore as fuck, knowing that my muscles will chill, but it'll take a hot shower and copious amounts of stretching and foam rolling to get there. I hobble to the dresser, pull on enough clothes so that I'm decent and move through the door, make my slow way downstairs.

Roxie's in the kitchen, sitting up at one of the stools, coloring while—

Tiffany stands at the stove.

Christ.

Because...not his girlfriend.

I press my tongue to the roof of my mouth.

Then exhale, long and slow.

Easy now.

"Mom!" Rox shouts and clambers down fast enough that I lurch toward her, toward my baby who's just had surgery.

Which sends a sharp enough pain through my side and back and shoulder and hips that I freeze, breath hissing out between my teeth.

Meanwhile my daughter—circling back to her just having had *surgery*—bounds over to me and throws her arms around my middle. "Hi, Mom."

I ignore the pain and smile down at her, squeezing her gently in return. "I guess this means you're feeling good, baby girl?"

"Yup," she says, nodding vigorously. "Tiff made me pancakes and brought me a new coloring book. Look"—she bounds over and picks it up—"it has Spiderman on it."

"So, it does," I say softly, glancing over at Tiff, whose expression is unreadable.

"Can I make you some pancakes, Brit?" she asks, holding up

the bowl like it's a peace offering. "I still have some batter left."

"As delicious as that sounds," I tell her, not wanting to hurt her feelings. "It's not a Cheat Day."

"Mom follows a special diet to make her strong," Rox announces, climbing back onto her stool.

"Oh wow," Tiff says, bringing the bowl to the sink and washing it. "That must be why she plays so well." Her gaze comes back to mine. "I saw the game last night. You were great."

Warmth in my belly.

Because even when I hated her because I thought she was in a relationship with Stefan, I still knew she was nice.

And she's *still* nice, offering to cook me breakfast (or brunch or pancakes for lunch) and coming over to spend time with Roxie.

Which reminds me.

"Thanks," I tell her then tilt my head to the hallway. "Have a second?"

Her brows draw together, but she sets the bowl down and nods. "Of course."

I ruffle Rox's hair. "Be right back, munchkin, and then will you show me your coloring?"

"Yup," she says, fully focused on filling in the outline of Spidey saving a school bus.

Tiff steps out into the hall, and I follow her, moving out of earshot of Rox in the kitchen.

"Is everything okay?" she asks, brow furrowed, hands fussing with the hem of her sweatshirt.

"Everything's great," I tell her. "I just...I was wondering how you and Stefan connected?"

The vee between her brows deepens.

"I mean," I ask, "did he get a referral for you from a company?"

Her teeth press into her bottom lip and worry crosses her face, and...I realize how that sounds.

Like I'm going to report her.

Or get her fired.

Or...well, *shit*.

"Sorry," I say quickly, words coming in rapid succession. "I don't mean to insinuate anything. At all. It's just...you're awesome with Roxie, and I travel a lot, as you know."

She smiles.

"It's about time for me to get my own Tiffany for when it's my custody time," I tell her. "So, I thought I'd ask you first."

The tension leaves her frame and she tilts her head to the side, warm brown eyes holding mine, studying me for a long moment. "You know," she finally says, "I'd be happy to help out on your weeks too."

"Really?" I ask.

She shrugs. "I love Roxie, and I already know her routine. It'd be easy enough."

Relief blooms in my belly. Still—

"I wasn't trying to pressure you into it," I tell her. "And I'll pay you separately from Stefan of course, if you really do have the time, and—" I chuckle—"the wherewithal to keep up with her during my weeks too."

Tiff grins. "She keeps me busy, that's for sure, but I don't mind."

Keeps her busy.

More like runs her ragged.

I hold back my wince. "Seriously, though, I totally understand if your schedule doesn't allow—"

She settles her hand onto my arm and exhales deeply. Then murmurs, "The truth is that money's a little tight right now, and tuition is coming due. And"—she shrugs again—"I really do love Rox, so I think if I picked up those other times, we'd both be doing each other a favor."

She sounds genuine enough that I'm starting to think that too. "As long as you're sure."

She nods.

I fix her in place with a glare. "And you'll let me know if it becomes too much with school?"

"I can do that." She drops her arm, pulls out her cell. "Let's exchange contacts and we can coordinate, yeah?"

I take her number down, give her mine then squeeze her arm. "Thanks, Tiff, I really owe you one."

"You don't owe me any—"

"Mom!"

She smiles, tilts her head toward the kitchen. "Speaking of keeping us busy." Her smile grows. "I'll just finish cleaning up and head out. I have a test to study for."

"You can take off now," I tell her. "I've got the dishes."

Her brow lifts. "I'll clean up and then head out," she says again, albeit more firmly.

Backbone.

Yeah, she and I are going to get along just fine.

Still, if she really *does* have a test to study for, I should—

"Mom!"

Tiff grins.

I sigh. Know that Rox is about to *keep me busy.*

"Fine," I mock grumble. "You win. You can wash the dishes."

Tiff salutes and we turn for the kitchen.

"Moooom!" Rox hollers, drawing my moniker out to approximately seven syllables.

"Coming, baby!" I holler back, unable to smother my bemused smile.

"Queen Rox calls," Tiff says, tone light, but as we start to move down the hall, something crosses her face and she slows to a stop.

"What is it?" I ask when she doesn't say anything.

Her chest rises and falls on a breath. "You asked how Stefan and I met."

I study her, wonder why her expression has gone more than a little serious. "Yeah, honey, I did." I bump her shoulder with mine, curious for sure, but not if it's a painful topic. I can be patient...and pry it out of her later. "But, truly, it doesn't matter to me."

She makes a face.

"I solemnly swear," I say lightly. "I trust his judgment. And you," I add, not wanting her to think that just because Stefan cleared it, I'd let anyone around my kid. Plus, she's been around long enough that I trust her too.

I wouldn't have allowed Rox to spend so much time with her if I didn't.

"Thanks," she says quietly. "That means a lot." A breath. "But I thought you should know—"

"*Mom!*"

"Roxie. Christ," I mutter. "Sorry, Tiff, but I should—"

"We met at a cancer support group," she blurts.

I freeze. "Oh," I whisper, all but skidding to a halt, guilt eating at my insides. "I'm sorry, honey. Stefan's a good resource to have when it comes to that. After everything he went through with his mom, I know that he can give you some great advice—"

She frowns, opens her mouth.

"*MOM!*"

"Jesus, Rox!" I call, moved past amused with my little munchkin and drifting straight into irritated. "I *said* I'll be right there." Then I turn back to Tiff. "What is it, honey?"

Her expression is unfathomable.

And I don't know her well enough yet, so I can't tell if she wants to talk, or wants to run away.

In the end, she does neither, just reaches over and squeezes my arm again. "I'd better get to those dishes. I've got an essay to write this afternoon."

"I—"

She walks into the kitchen.

I follow her, and Queen Rox quickly dominates my attention, and...I let the thread of conversation go.

But I promise myself I'm going to get to the bottom of what is making her sad.

I'm just...

Going to do it after I get Stefan to spill his guts.

Twenty-Seven

Stefan

"I can't advise delaying treatment," my doctor says, turning the monitor so I can see the scan on it.

"You said it's smaller," I point out.

"That is true." He touches the tip of his pen to a section of the screen. "This is looking great. I wouldn't do anything further on it at this time, but this"—he taps a different spot—"this needs to be taken care of, Stefan, and it needs to be sooner rather than later."

"I'm not saying that I'm not going to *do* the treatment," I say. "I just need a little more time."

Like when Brit is on that extended road trip coming up, and I can get it done and recover before she gets back.

"These kinds of things aren't served well by taking more time," he says.

My temple starts throbbing, and I sigh. "I know." I meet his eyes. "Believe me, I *know*."

My doctor studies me. "But you're still going to take that time, aren't you?"

Basically, *you're still going to be an idiotic dumbfuck,*

aren't you?

I get where he's coming from—absolutely, I do.

I lived and breathed this reality for years...for the *last* year.

So, the short answer is yes.

I *am* going to be a dumbfuck.

But just for a little while.

Then I'll be smart again.

"Roxie needs me," I say. "She's recovering from surgery and I need to be there for her."

My doctor shakes his head. "Look," he says. "I understand where you're coming from, but you need to remember that kids are resilient, so while I think it's admirable to want to be there for your daughter"—he clicks his pen, tucks it into his pocket—"I also want you to consider that might not be the real reason you're hitting the brakes now."

Irritation begins to burn in my gut.

But he's still talking.

"So, you need to think whether if this delay is really because you're worried about your daughter? Or if it's another reason..."

I brace, thinking he's seen through me, that he knows exactly how long I want the delay and for what reason, especially as he seems to war with what he wants to say.

And I know he knows it's not just about Rox.

That it's about Brit.

And, fuck, I can't do this.

I need to go. I've barely had the strength to do what I need there—and I'm failing at it, considering I fucked her the night before, considering I told her—

That throb in my temple grows.

Considering I've fought to keep my distance from her for the last months...

And failed utterly.

My doctor sighs as I'm sitting in that failure.

Then...he just drops it on me. "I think it's less about you needing to be there for Roxie and more that you're scared of what the outcome of the treatment might be"—he presses a few buttons on the keyboard and the screen goes black—"and what the journey to that recovery will look like."

Hard.

It's going to look hard, I know that. I—

Well, I fucking *know* it.

But—

I'm not afraid of hard.

It's why I made a living playing professional hockey.

It's why I've made it *this* far.

I just—

He settles his hand on my shoulder. "Think about what I said." He squeezes lightly, releases me. "And then keep the appointment."

A nod and then he's gone, disappearing into the hall, the door clicking closed behind him.

Leaving me alone in the patient room, sitting on a paper-covered table, stewing over being called a coward.

I sit there for a long time.

And then go out to the front desk and I reschedule my treatment.

———

"Again, Dad!" Rox says and I toss the pizza dough up in the air.

We both look up, watching the disc of dough spin around and around.

It falls back down and I catch it before any pizza catastrophes can happen, smoothing it back out onto the peel. "Want to do sauce, Roxie girl?"

She reaches for the bowl of homemade sauce and begins to spoon it onto the crust, plopping some in the middle and using the back of the spoon to smooth it around and around like I taught her. "Is this the special one for Mom?" she asks.

SCORED

"Yup," I say. "Veggies and vegan cheese for Mom. Olives and pineapple for us."

A combination that's...disgusting, likely to the outside world, but something that Roxie and I both enjoy.

"I love pineapple!" she says, darting a hand forward and trying to sneak out a slice of pineapple from the bowl I have ready for topping.

"I know," I reply lightly, letting her grab a couple of pieces before nudging the container out of reach. "We'll put Mom's in the oven when she gets home so it's hot for her. Sound good?"

"Yup," she says chomping on the fruit. "Are we going to wait for her to cook ours?"

"Depends." I start spreading cheese over the sauce.

"On what?" she asks, head tilting to the side, ponytail swinging behind her in a way that has my heart squeezing.

Because it reminds me of her mom.

And the conversation with my doctor.

And thinking about Brit finally being done with my dumb ass.

And...about not being able to be here with Rox, making pizza and pretending not to see her stealing more pineapple.

"Dad?"

"Depends on how hungry you are."

Rox freezes with a pineapple halfway to her mouth. "I'm not *that* hungry."

My lips twitch. Because she'd eaten half a pineapple in the last five minutes.

I finish with the cheese, start in on the olives. "I bet."

"So, we'll wait for Mom?" she asks.

"Sounds good to me," I tell her, snagging the remaining pineapple and spreading it on top of the cheese and olives.

"Dad?" she asks in between bites of fruit.

"Yeah?"

"Are you and Mom going to live together again?"

I nearly drop the bowl.

Luckily, I manage to keep hold of it long enough to set it in the sink, to turn on the water, to add soap, to fill it up.

Delaying.

Because my daughter is too fucking smart.

Because I'm a dumbass.

Because...I don't know what the fuck I'm doing.

Her arms wrapping around my waist make me jump. "It's okay if you're not," she says quietly, but I see the sadness in her eyes before she deliberately tries for something positive. "Teddy's parents are divorced and he gets two Christmases."

Or maybe calculating.

Christ.

Kids.

"Will I get two Christmases too?" she asks innocently.

"I—"

"And birthdays? And—"

The garage door rumbles open.

Thank. Fucking. God.

Brit's early.

Which isn't like her. She's always is the first on the ice, the last off it, and then does cardio and weights and—

"—sleepovers?"

Sweet Christ.

Not double the amount of sleepovers.

That should be enough motivation to stay married for any sane person.

Focus.

"That sounds like Mom's home, want to go check?" I nod toward the second circle of dough. "I'll start on her pizza and then we can all eat together."

"Okay!" Rox says and clambers down from the chair we pulled up to the counter so she could properly commence her pizza topping skills (or her pineapple eating skills, such it is). Her footsteps echo from the hall and I hear the door to the garage open, the sound of an engine, the rumbling of the metal panel sliding down. "Mom's home!" she calls, and I grin.

And start working on the second pizza as I hear Brit's voice ringing toward me.

It's cheerful and bright, as always.

But when she steps into the kitchen, it only takes one look at her face for me to know that something is seriously wrong.

TWENTY-EIGHT

BRIT

"I'm surprised," Frankie says from next to me, crouched on one knee on the ice next to me as we scoop up pucks, toss them into the plastic basket they're stored in.

"Surprised at what?" I ask, shooing him away.

He stays after practice to give me some extra training—the least I can do is clean up after myself.

"That you're only going for one bucket today," he says.

My stomach clenches and I can't shove down the bolt of guilt that slides through my middle. Maybe I should stay a little longer, practice just a bit more, keep going until I'm perfect and—

He settles his hand on my shoulder. "I'm *pleasantly* surprised, Brit."

The knot in my gut loosens, and I exhale. "Stefan and Roxie are making pizzas."

His face changes, and I know with just that much, he gets it. "That's good, honey," he says. "I was wondering how long it would take for you two to work things out."

I wince.

Does fucking and exchanging romantic words *really* count as working it out?

Especially when there's so much that we haven't discussed, haven't come to terms with, haven't—

"You know," Frankie says, coming down onto his other knee, not letting me shoo him away from the pucks this time, "I always thought that you'd be right here."

"On the ice?" I ask. "I know you're intuitive, Frankie, but that's not much of a stretch."

His smile is a flash of white. "I meant training the next guy."

I freeze, fingers wrapped around a frozen disc of rubber. "Wh-what?"

"I always figured when you retire from the crease that you'd step into coaching," he says matter-of-factly.

Just dropping a bomb.

Coaching?

I still.

That's not—

"You've had a good run, Banana"—his lips curve—"but have you thought about what you're going to do when you're done?" He fixes me with a stare. "I mean *really* done, not that Michael Jordan retire and come back nonsense you pulled a couple of seasons back."

"Frankie."

"Not pressuring you." He tosses a puck into the bucket. "Just...food for thought."

"I..."

He stills, and I want to run from the thoughts in my head, want to ignore the fear that unleashes in me—what am I without hockey?

Who am I if I'm not Brit Plantain, the first woman to play in the NHL?

Who am I without this team behind me?

Who am I without Stefan? Without Rox?

And why is it that the last two questions are the ones that really strike fear into my heart?

All of that is running through my mind as we kneel there, Frankie beside me, not pushing me to talk or move or—

"I should let you get back to your grand kids," I say instead of acknowledging his statements.

Because he watches them at their karate class these evenings and that's more important than me having an existential crisis—

"Brit," he says softly.

"I know they're testing for their new belts soon," I tell him. "You'll want to make sure you see them practice."

"Brit," he says again, still soft. But this time, he waits.

For me to look at him.

I don't want to.

I *want* to drop my mask back down and skate back over to the net and take a hundred more shots so I don't have to think about my marriage dissolving and my role in it, how I might have been so fucking focused on my career and passion that I ruined my relationship, how I might not have been what Stefan wanted or needed.

But he said—

Sweet words aren't actions.

So, I want to avoid thinking that I might be becoming the same person for Roxie—not enough, too focused on my own stuff, too—

Well, just not good enough.

And I sure as shit *want* to stop worrying about who I'll be without hockey and just...*do* hockey.

Get lost in the rush. Solve any problems in the locker room or on the ice or with my guys and *their* partners and—

I've been doing exactly that for the last couple of months— okay, well...if I'm being completely honest with myself, I've been doing it for the last few years...

Scared to let go and move on to the next stage of my life.

Scared *not* to.

Woman enough? Or too much?

A good mom? How *can* I be good when I'm training so much and traveling so often? How can I be when I miss Muffins with Moms and am not in town to help Rox with her book report? How can I be a good example as a strong woman if I just give up my career?

It's all messed up and terrifying and...it's been easier to stick with what I know.

And all of that means I'm no closer to solving the shit in my head, my heart, my soul.

But I do finally find the courage to look up at Frankie. "You're not ready," he says. "And that's okay." His mouth kicks up. "Just try not to be too hard on yourself until you are."

I suck in a breath, hold it for a long time.

Then exhale, managing to keep my tone light when I ask, "Have you met me?"

He doesn't buy that lightness, I can see it on his face, but he doesn't call me on it, just straightens with a groan and says, "When you're ready to be done, new opportunities will arise. Some may be shit." His lips twitch. "But one of those might be gold." He fixes me with a stare. "Like being the *Gold's* new goalie coach."

I suck in a breath.

But he's still talking.

"When you're ready," he repeats, and then snags the basket of pucks, carries it over to the boards, climbing through the open door. "See you tomorrow after the game," he calls over his shoulder before disappearing down the hall.

I look around the empty rink as though that will give me answers, and unsurprisingly, I don't find any, so I...

Push it all down as I get up onto my skates, move through that open door, walking down the hall to the locker room.

I ignore the banana in my stall—swear to God, a woman talks about her love of the yellow, penis-shaped fruit *one* time and all of a sudden it's a catchphrase.

Fucking hockey players.

Fucking locker room razzing.

Fucking brain that is all twisted up.

Ugh.

I change and shower, shoot the shit with the guys, and then—ignoring all manner of knowing looks from my teammates, all of whom are clearly far too familiar with my routine, far more familiar than they should be—I walk out of the practice facility, intent on my car.

So intent that I don't realize what's happening at first.

So intent that I don't see the man coming up behind me.

TWENTY-NINE

STEFAN

"Wine?" I murmur as Brit comes out of Roxie's room, blowing her bangs out of her eyes, giving me that beleaguered look of a parent whose kid. Will. Not. Just. Fucking. Sleep.

"It's not a Cheat Day," she says with a soft groan, starting to push the bangs off her forehead.

"Tomorrow is," I point out. "And I think Rebecca would okay a single glass of wine after dealing with Queen Rox."

Her lips twitch.

"Isn't it also good for your blood pressure?" I tease.

She grins then shakes her head, ponytail swinging exactly like Roxie's had a few hours ago as we'd made pizzas. "You're a bad influence, Stefan Barie."

"I happen to think I'm a very *good* influence," I say as we walk into the family room, extending a hand, showing her the wine glass I already knew she'd accept sitting on the coffee table.

"The best," she agrees, moving forward, snatching it up, and drinking greedily.

I chuckle, pick up my own beer.

But then she lowers her glass, shoulders slumping.

"What is it?" I ask softly.

"What the fuck are we doing?"

Her tone is so forlorn that I still, guilt jabbing. "What do you mean?" I rasp.

She sighs, sets the glass on the table. "I mean, you're here. With Rox. Making us all pizzas. Watching dumb kids' TV shows. Staying while I get her in bed."

It's like I'm suddenly in a room filled with dangerous animals —rattlesnakes and grizzlies and black widows, all just waiting to attack. "So?"

"So, we're divorced—"

"Not technically."

Her eyes flash. "You served me with papers. We're hammering out joint property and custody."

"I told my attorney to give you anything you wanted."

She jerks slightly then shakes her head. "You know that's not what I'm talking about. You hated me—"

I move toward her, cupping her face in my hands. "I never could hate you, baby."

Lids sliding closed, but not before I see the disbelief, the hurt, the sadness in those chocolate-brown depths. "It sure seemed like you did."

Because it was a convenient fucking excuse.

Because...there *was* anger there and resentment.

"I was ready to start our life together," I admit. "I want to have more kids. I want to travel and have a life that doesn't revolve around hockey. I want you, but—"

Her eyes open. "I'm not ready to let it go."

That...well, it fucking hurts.

That hockey is more of a priority to her than our life together after it.

But I know it's not fair.

I wrestled with my own decision about retiring for far longer than Brit has, and my playing didn't affect our family planning.

It's not that I don't love Roxie, don't love the work we do to help kids in need.

But...I want more.

I want a little girl who looks like Brit.

I want a boy with my eyes.

I want Rox to have siblings.

I want our house to be full of chaos—even more than what Rox and the Gold family create.

"I know," I tell her gently.

"And," she whispers. "I don't know when I will be."

"It's not fair for me to expect you to give it up," I tell her, dropping my forehead against hers. "I know that now. I knew that then." My smile is wry and self-deprecating. "But I wasn't thinking clearly."

Her eyes widen.

"I made a mistake," I say. "I love you and I let all of my resentment fester and eat at me."

And...I let the news I received just before the shooting push me over the edge.

Let it push me into making the dumbest fucking decision of my life.

"A mistake," she whispers.

I nudge her down onto the couch, sit next to her, and because I can't stand the distance between us, I pull her into my arms.

"A mistake?" she whispers again.

"Yeah, baby." And I'm so drunk on the feel of holding her, of having this moment with her, so high on the night together as a family, doing nothing special but something incredibly important because we're spending time with each other, that I miss the deadly edge to her tone.

"A fucking mistake, Stefan?"

And because this one is paired with her shoving at my chest, pushing me away from her—and doing it hard enough that it gets through my thick, dumb skull— I finally clue in. "Baby—"

"A mistake," She pops up to her feet in an angry, jerky movement, thrusting a hand through her ponytail, clenching the fingers tightly in her fist. "A fucking *mistake*."

I try again. "Baby—"

"Do you know what you put Roxie through?" she asks, dropping her hand but sounding like she's grinding her teeth. "What you put *me* through?" She picks up her wineglass, drains it in one long gulp. Then takes the bottle I left next to it, fills it to the brim, starts draining it again. "I thought—" She clamps her lips together, shakes her head.

"You thought what?"

Another long gulp.

"Brit."

More wine being guzzled, enough that I snag the glass from her, set it on the table.

"*Brit.*"

She sighs, looks away. "I'm not a good mom," she whispers. "I'm not home making handprint crafts, not bringing goodie bags to school for her birthday."

"Baby—"

"And I'm not a good wife. I'm obsessed with hockey, spend too much time away from home, too much time training, too much time focused on my career instead of home with—"

I touch her jaw. "I love that you're so passionate about hockey, baby."

"Only you don't," she whispers. "You just said you resented it—"

"I—"

The words stopper up in my throat because...she's not wrong.

It's just...she's not entirely right.

"It wasn't you. It was me."

That has her freezing, brows shooting up nearly to her hairline. "It wasn't *you*. It was *me*? Seriously?" She shoves me away, picks up the wine glass again. "You're using that fucking line right now."

"It's n-not a line," I stammer, heart filling with ice. This isn't my friend, my wife, my lover. This is Brit Plantain, the fearsome hockey player who will let nothing stand in her way.

Even me.

"Bullshit," she snaps. "Do you know how long I wrestled with all of that—the pressure of mom and wife, of doing my fucking job, of being woman enough for a man like you? And thinking all this time that I failed, that I *wasn't* good enough or pretty enough or attractive enough or feminine enough. Thinking that I was fucking up every single aspect of my life, and now—" She throws a hand out, sloshing wine over the rim of the glass. "Now you're telling me you made a mistake. A *mistake!*"

I snag the glass from her again, setting it on the table before reaching for her.

Only, she bats my hands away. "Don't touch me."

Normally, I wouldn't push this, but the pain in her eyes, the fragile way she's holding herself...I know I can't let that distance remain, not when I've let it grow and burn and fester inside her.

So, I ignore her and draw her close, pinning her arms down at her sides, tucking her against me. "It's not bullshit when I say that I haven't so much as looked at another woman since you've been in my life. You're it for me, baby."

"Then why—" Her voice breaks. "Why did you do this to us?"

I still, stomach knotting, bile burning the back of my throat.

And I know...I know I have to tell her.

All of it.

Not the half-truths and easy explanations.

The last card I've been holding close.

The one that's—

Well, the one that was the sole reason I ever considered leaving the woman I loved.

I open my mouth. "Baby, I—"

And the doorbell rings.

THIRTY

BRIT

Finally.

    Finally, I felt like we were getting somewhere.

    And the fucking doorbell rings.

"Ignore it," I whisper.

Stefan is so far from the confident, self-assured man I know as he stumbles through his next words. "I—sweetheart, it's not what you think—or not *all* that you think—"

The doorbell goes again, paired with a knock this time.

And...fuck.

I sigh.

Because we live in a gated community. Because it's eight-thirty at night, and if someone is knocking on my door, it's not because they're selling vacuums. It's likely important.

"I...well, I—"

The bell rings a third time.

It's likely important *and* whoever's on the other side is going to wake up my daughter if they keep going on like this.

And then I'll *never* get her to go back to sleep.

Something that Stefan seems to realize at the same time. "I'll get it," he mutters, bending and snagging the glass of wine from the table and passing it back to me. "Drink. Relax. Then we'll talk."

I nod, relieved that he seems to be intent to keep talking, and lift the glass to my lips, taking a sip of the crisp, citrusy white that's my favorite wine. It's from a local winery, the proprietor now the owner of the Oakland Eagles and Rome's future father-in-law.

But that only holds my attention for a split second.

Because then there's a loud *thud* in the hall, the sound of flesh meeting flesh, a grunt, and—

"Fuck!" I hiss, plunking the glass on the table and jumping to my feet, sprinting out of the family room, turning the corner, and—

Skidding to a halt.

What the actual fuck?

Dan—my big brother and only living biological relative, my brother who works for the FBI and is never home, my brother who is not supposed to get in until tomorrow is—

"Stop!" I cry, running toward the pair of them. Well, toward my brother who's got Stefan pinned against the wall, his hand wrapped around his throat, and murder in his eyes.

"You're fucking in her *house*, asshole?" Dan is grinding out. "You're standing in her house in fucking sweatpants and bare feet after all the shit you pulled on her? Fucking *really*?"

I inhale sharply through my nose.

My brother drops his face even closer, growling out words I can't hear.

"Dan," I say sharply before this can get even more out of hand. "Let go of my husband."

"*Ex*-husband," he says, head swiveling toward me as though he knew I was there the whole time.

Hell, he's an FBI agent. He probably *did* know I was there from the moment I stepped into the hall.

"Dan," I sigh. "You're early."

"And you're taking up with this asshole again?" he snaps, still not releasing Stefan.

"You're not supposed to be here until tomorrow." I move toward him, warning Stefan to stay still with my eyes. He's not fighting back, not because he can't throw down in a fight—he can —but because Dan is my brother and I love him, and—

He won't hurt someone who's important to me.

"I caught an earlier flight," Dan says, eyes flashing as he glances over at me.

"I'm glad you're here," I say. "But I'd rather you don't commit murder in my hallway."

Some of the ice leaves his eyes, and his mouth curves up just the slightest bit at the edges as he shrugs. "I can make the body disappear."

God. My brother.

He's...

Something else.

"You owe me a hug," I say softly.

The rest of the ice disappears and he drops his hand from Stefan's throat, shoulders relaxing, big body becoming more teddy bear and less murderous FBI agent. "Come here," he mutters, wrapping me in his arms and kissing the top of my head. "Missed you, kid."

Warmth in my belly.

My soul settling.

My big bro is here and everything will be all right.

"Missed you too," I whisper.

He lifts his brows. "Want to fill me in on what's happening here?"

I don't even pretend to not know what he's talking about, just lift up on tiptoe and press a kiss to his cheek. "It's complicated." I drop back down onto my heels.

He shoots me a droll look.

"No, Laila after all?" I ask, inquiring after his wife—also an agent—instead of letting him pursue a conversational gambit I'm not ready to traverse.

Stefan and I had sex.

We're talking.

We're...coexisting peacefully.

I'm the only woman for him.

He has a secret.

My head starts throbbing.

Dan brushes a finger over my temple. "She got called away on a case."

"Darn."

His mouth curves into a ghost of a smile. "You're just saying that because you want to team up and destroy me in *Ticket to Ride*."

"Maybe." He grins now, though that disappears when he looks over his shoulder.

I follow his stare, see that Stefan has come close.

Murder is back on the table, folks.

"Did you eat?" I ask, distracting my brother in one of the few effective ways I have—through his stomach. "Stefan made pizza."

He finally settles, his expression relaxing. "With homemade dough?"

"Do I make any other kind of pizza?" Stefan asks dryly.

Dan scowls, but it's more big brother and less I'm going to kill the person who hurt my sister. "I don't know," he mutters. "You've done a lot of shit that doesn't make any sense over the last year."

"I—"

"Uncle Dan?"

We all freeze at the sound of Roxie's voice then turn as one, though only Stefan and I do it with quiet groans.

"Uncle Dan!"

Roxie's face transforms—sleepy confusion into blatant excitement—and then she's moving, pounding down the stairs, running over to us, throwing herself in Dan's arms.

"Careful, baby girl," he says, gently scooping her up. "You're supposed to be taking it easy."

"I'm a fast recover-er," she announces, throwing her arms around him.

Dan grins. "I can see that."

"Are you gonna eat Dad's pizza?"

Dan glances over at Stefan, mulish expression in place. "Yeah," he mutters.

"I helped make it."

Dan—my big, annoying, giant of a brother—chills, face softening as he carefully maneuvers Rox to his shoulders and takes off for the kitchen. "Well then, I'm *definitely* going to eat that pizza. I bet it's extra delicious because you helped."

"I put lots and *lots* of pineapple."

Dan freezes, glancing over his shoulder at me, brows lifted.

"Not my fault," I tell her. "Blame..." I name a famous YouTuber whose recipes Rox loves to try out.

He makes a face, but his tone is even. "Well, it's a good thing that I love pineapple, isn't it?"

"Just not on pizza," Stefan whispers.

I still, tilt my head up, eyes meeting his.

He brushes a hand over my cheek. "We'll talk later," he murmurs. A tilt of his head toward the kitchen. "Go be with your brother. I'll get the guest room ready for him."

The guest room where he'd been staying.

"You're going home?" I ask, oddly disappointed.

Fingers sliding into my ponytail, tilting my head back, brushing his mouth over mine.

"No, baby," he murmurs. "I'm moving back in."

THIRTY-ONE

STEFAN

"Can you grab down the glasses?" Brit asks early the next morning, nodding toward the top shelf of the cabinet.

"How much are you planning on drinking?" I tease, moving close to her and reaching up, snagging the wine glasses down one by one. "Was the bottle you finished off last night not enough?"

While she and Dan, Rox and I all stayed up way too late.

Eating pizza—well, Dan had eaten it anyway, the rest of us had warm cookies that Brit made from some refrigerated dough she threw in the oven.

Drinking—wine for Brit, beer for Dan and me, orange juice with a little sparkling apple cider mixed in for Rox.

Catching up—over kid appropriate board games and then, when Rox had finally passed out and I tucked her back into bed, over a brutal matchup of *Ticket to Ride.*

Dan was the champion.

We were all slightly buzzed.

And sleep had taken us the moment our heads hit the pillows —or at least it had taken Brit and me.

Now we're up, Rox and Dan have gone off on an Uncle Adventure, according to the note Brit's brother had left on the counter.

"It's Book Club today," she says, going to the fridge and pulling some fruit and vegetables, a package of presliced cheese, a wheel of brie and some jam.

Charcuterie.

These women are obsessed.

"What's Mandy bringing?" I ask, stomach rumbling softly.

"A dessert board."

I actually feel the drool pooling in my mouth. "And Sara?" I ask.

Brit's lips kick up. "Mimosa fixings."

Okay, that's less exciting. I open my mouth—

"The other girls are bringing seven-layer dip, chocolate lasagna, homemade sourdough and butter, and some sort of fall-themed soup," she recites, ticking the items off on her fingers. "All of which are reserved for those who actually read the book."

"What's the title?" I ask. "I'll read it right now."

She laughs, shakes her head, starts slicing vegetables, arranging them neatly on the cutting board. Then sighs, lays the knife down.

"What?" I ask softly, moving closer, unable to stay away.

"You know what," she replies, just as softly.

I open my mouth, close it.

She sighs. "I know," she whispers, dropping her hands to the counter, hanging her head. "We have shit timing. Last night with Dan. This morning with the girls showing at the door any moment."

"It'll hold," I murmur. "You have tonight off. After Rox and Dan go to bed, we'll talk."

Stillness in her body for several long heartbeats.

Then she sighs again, nods. "Yeah," she whispers. "We'll talk tonight."

"Okay, baby," I murmur. "Now"—I wrap my arms around her from behind—"am I slicing or arranging?"

More stillness.

More tension.

Then she exhales and smiles. "You're arranging," she says. "Last time I got so much shit for quote, 'Cutting up a bunch of yummy shit and dumping it on a cutting board.'" She tosses her hands up, shakes her head. "So what if it's not pretty? It's delicious and in bite-sized pieces and—"

"God, I love you."

It's a blurt—a complete and total word vomit at wholly the wrong time.

We haven't talked.

There's a fucking wealth of shit between us that we need to work out.

And her friends are going to come barreling in through the front door any second now.

Her fingers tighten on the knife, and she slowly turns my way.

Fuck, she's going to kill me.

I put her through too much.

And she's finally snapped.

The knife goes skittering across the counter, clatters into the sink, and then her arms are around me, her mouth is coming to mine, and—

I grunt as she jumps, legs going around my waist, tongue slipping between my lips, hands diving into my hair.

And then I'm not thinking about conversations that need to happen, secrets that need to be told.

I'm *feeling*.

Her gorgeous body against mine, the sweet taste of her tongue as it glides over mine, hair on my skin, tits pressed to my chest.

Mine. All fucking *mine*.

And that I almost gave this up, that I took it this far, almost to the point of no return, that I thought I could live without it, without her—

I had lost my fucking mind.

And I need to beg her for forgiveness, thank her for being willing to at least hear me out—

She pulls at my hair. "Stop thinking and kiss me back."

So...

I do.

Because if I've learned anything from my idiocy over the last year, it's that the future is fragile, changeable, can unravel into a thousand strands of nothing.

Sometimes it's best to just leap into the present and—

Grab on.

I spin around, settling her onto the counter, not giving her a second to breathe, to think, to change her mind. I rip her shirt over her head, toss it aside, and immediately undo the clasp on her bra, sliding the material down her arms, dropping it to the floor.

Breasts and taut nipples that call for my mouth.

But I don't get to taste because she's reaching for my shirt, yanking it up and off. Then shoving at my sweats, my underwear, freeing my dick in one strong push of the material.

I step out of it, bend for her again, but she's moving, reacting, taking what she wants.

Fucking. *Love.* Her.

Slender fingers pushing down her leggings, her underwear, using one foot and then the other to drag them off her ankles, to kick the stretchy black Lycra free.

And then *she's* free.

Touching her fingers to my chest, to the spot over my heart, holding my eyes. "I love you too," she whispers.

A dagger to the heart.

Guilt sweeping through me.

I open my mouth to tell her, to explain—fuck the timing— but then her hand is dropping away and she's turning, giving me a view of an ass that is so lush and curvy and beautiful that my knees actually wobble.

I lock them so I don't end up on my own ass, cock tightening, throbbing, my hand wrapping around it tightly, stroking up and down, up and down.

She bends forward, rests her elbows on the counter.

Then glances over her shoulder at me.

"Fuck me, honey," she orders softly. "Deep and hard and fast. Fuck me like we used to. Fuck me like we *have* to. Fuck—"

I move before I'm fully processing it, kicking her feet apart, barely having the control to swipe my fingers through her cunt, thankfully finding it dripping, because I'm already shifting, bending my knees a little, gripping her hip, my slick fingers sliding on her skin as I—

"*Fuck*," I groan.

"*Fuck*," *she* groans.

And then I'm inside, deep in that pussy, its wet, hot clasp nearly sending me to the floor again.

My head's spinning.

My dick is ready to explode.

My heart...well, it's focused only on Brit.

Committing this to memory—her soft moans as I pull out and slide back in, the way her nails claw against the granite for purchase, the flex of her hips as she pushes back against me.

And all the while, I'm fucking her deep. I'm fucking her fast. I'm fucking her hard.

Flutters are my first indication, teasing the head of my cock, stroking along the shaft, growing firmer, more intense, harder until—

"Oh God!"

There.

I press a hand between her shoulder blades, forcing her down onto the counter, gripping her hip, and pounding into her.

Because she's close.

Because she needs it.

Because if she doesn't come right fucking *now*, I'm going to without her—

"Stefan!" She bucks, arches back hard.

But I don't relent, can't relent, can't ever let her go.

"Oh!" she screams. "Oh my God. I—"

And then her pussy grips me hard enough that I see stars and a wave of dizziness sweeps over me and...

I come apart with her, pleasure bursting through every inch of me as I stroke once, twice, three times more, my groan loud and deep and mixing with hers as I slow, grinding deep, riding the rhythmic aftershocks of her orgasm until we're both spent.

Which is the moment that my knees give way.

And also the moment...

The doorbell rings.

Thirty-Two

BRIT

So, choosing sex over a conversation probably wasn't the best course of action.

But it had been...delicious.

The orgasm and the way he held me, the way he lost control, leaving me no doubt of him being attracted to me.

Cooling the edges of the discomfort that had crept in over the last months, soothing the doubt in myself and insecurity about my body. Making the worries about getting older, parts sagging, skin and flesh not as taut or bouncy as it had once been, disappear off into space.

I'm different.

What if all of this—Stefan leaving, my marriage imploding—what if it all stemmed from me changing, from our love unable to keep up?

What if...

I was the problem.

And not *us*.

That thought had eaten at me for months.

And now to know it wasn't my body, wasn't *me*—

Well, I can handle not being the *sole* problem in our relationship.

The only trouble left is that I don't know Stefan's half yet.

Sex and mimosas. Book club and more time with Dan. Drinking too much, passing out, waking in the middle of the night to make love—more orgasms instead of talking.

Then Rox and Dan. Pregame prep.

And...now.

Two more days have passed, and Stefan and I are...playing make believe. Meanwhile, we haven't talked, not about whatever he's holding back from me, whatever is the truth underlying everything that pulled us apart.

We're just...slipping back into old patterns, old comforts, old routines.

The whistle trills and I yank myself back into focus.

Roxie is in the stands, Dan and Stefan sitting on either side of her. I need to play well—not just for the team, but for her and Dan. Show off for my ultimate fans in the stands.

Show off for—

Stefan.

Old patterns. Old comforts. Old routines.

My stomach tightens.

The guys line up for the face-off, and I push that away. I do what I'm best at—locking it down, focusing on hockey, getting ready to keep the puck out of the net.

The ref lets the biscuit drop and the centers go to battle, Ben winning it back into the corner.

The Sierra are on it in an instant, and then the war is on.

Fighting for every touch of the puck, every pass, every shot—

I grunt, push hard to the side, digging my edge in, ignoring the pain through my torso as I stretch my pad out, reach my glove up.

I hear the *smack* of the puck in my glove before I feel the sting across my palm, am clenching my fingers, closing around it, holding tight as I wait for the whistle.

Trill!

Thank God.

I straighten, give my side a break, toss the puck to the ref and buy some time for the pain to subside by taking a long swig of water. But as I set the bottle in the holder, my eyes drift up a few rows and I grin when I see Roxie up and dancing, Dan beside her, doing his goofy big brother jig that has Rox in stitches.

And I wince.

Not because of my side, my body revolting from all these years of sport.

But because I'm not there next to them, not dancing to the music blaring through the arena.

That I'm literally on the wrong side of the glass, so I *can't* do that.

My eyes drift to the side, and I see Stefan on his feet as well, but he's not dancing.

He's looking at me, concern rippling over his expression.

Worried about my side.

Meanwhile, he should be worried about my heart.

I always thought that you'd be right here.

Frankie's voice slides through my mind, and I freeze.

I'd always thought *right here* meant the crease, the ice, the locker room. Until Frankie had put the idea of coaching in my head.

No, until I'd lost everything.

Until I'd stood on the outside, looking in, missing out on my old life, my beautiful future.

The whistle blows and I jerk—

"You good, Brit?" the ref calls.

I inhale, force a smile, and wave at Rox who notices me looking, at Dan who nods encouragingly. My gaze slides back to Stefan's and my breath catches.

The outside looking in.

He's been that for a long time—ever since he retired and I kept playing.

And...I exhale.

I get it.

I do.

I think I finally do.

Because...soon enough I'm going to be on the other side of the glass, and—

"Brit?"

I exhale again, nod sharply to drop my helmet back down, and I feel the pieces inside me settle.

Soon enough.

But not now.

Then I turn to the ref who's skated over, grin at him through my mask. "Just waving to my fans," I tell him, moving into position.

The ref chuckles. "Can't rush that," he teases and then skates over to get ready for the puck drop.

I suck in a breath.

Roll my shoulders.

I crouch into position.

I...lock it down and focus on the game.

But all I can think is that maybe it's not *rushing* if I'm finally ready for it.

———

Roxie lost her battle with sleep halfway through the third period, so Dan and Stefan took her home.

I've just finished with my post-game shots, exercise, and stretches, and now I'm packing up and heading out.

Only...my best friends have other ideas.

They're on either side of the hallway as I come out of the locker room, arms crossed, mulish expressions in place, and I know there's no avoiding this conversation, as much as I want to.

They saw post-orgasm Brit at Book Club.

They saw Stefan at the game tonight, hanging in the hall,

softly saying goodbye with Rox sleeping in his arms, her head on his shoulder.

So, I don't bother trying to make it by them, trying to delay the inevitable.

I've done that enough—avoiding the discomfort, ostriching like the best of them.

"The training suite or somewhere else?" I ask.

Sara had clearly been expecting an argument because her mouth opens and closes and no words come out.

Mandy, though, recovers faster, tilting her head down the hall, turning and walking toward the training suite. I follow her without an argument, knowing that she'll have me contained in her space soon enough and there will likely be hell to pay.

I sigh.

Know that if I was her, I'd be doing the same thing.

We're family. They've given me far more space than I could have hoped for.

Now I've got to pay the piper.

I move into the training suite, walk over to my usual table, hopping up on the leather-covered surface and swinging my legs back and forth, back and forth as Sara strolls through the door, as Mandy closes it behind her.

They both cross over to me, Sara hopping up onto the table next to me, Mandy leaning on the one across from mine.

Boxing me in.

My mouth hitches up.

A play right out of the Nosy Brit handbook.

So, I decide not to make it hard on them.

"Stefan and I are back together."

The words are sure, steady, but the fact that I've actually said them out loud has my pulse speeding up.

Sara goes still next to me.

Mandy sucks in a breath. "Brit, honey," she begins after a moment. "He—"

"I know," I tell her. "And I know you guys are looking out for me, know that I would be doing the same for you if this was happening between you and Blane"—I turn to Sara—"or between you and Mike."

"Yeah," Mandy snaps. "I know you would. Which means that we're stopping you from making a giant mistake."

A giant mistake in getting back with him, in trying to make things work.

Stupid, giving in to the crap he put me through like a weak ass bitch.

Only...

It's not that simple.

"Mandy," Sara begins.

"No." Mandy shoves off the bench. "This is bullshit. He's spent the last year putting you through hell. He's dating a girl who's a good two decades younger than you, and bringing her around your kid—"

"Tiff is his nanny."

"—and making you feel like you're not good enough. Not woman enough." She throws up her hands. "*That's* bullshit. You're fucking amazing and that he doesn't see that, has to find his validation in someone else—"

"Tiffany isn't his girlfriend," I say a little louder. "She's his nanny."

Mandy freezes, drops her hands to her sides. "What?" she whispers.

"I saw what I wanted to see," I say softly. "But the truth is that it's not a girlfriend, not hockey, not me wanting to wait to have more kids or traveling all the time or even coming out of retirement that tore us apart."

Mandy comes back to the table across from me, demeanor softening.

Sara reaches out, takes my hand, and I feel my eyes sting. "So, what did, honey?"

I inhale, release it slowly. "The truth is that...I don't know all that tore us apart."

Mandy scowls. "Honey, I—"

"But I know enough, and I know what I want," I tell them. "And...I know there's something he's holding back, something that will make it all make sense. Something that pulled him away from me because..." I inhale. "He loves me. I know he does."

Sara's fingers convulse. "Of course he does," she murmurs. "He would be an idiot *not* to."

Mandy's eyes slide closed, shoulders rising and falling on a breath. Then she opens them, and finally I see the rage on my behalf turn into something else—the slightest bit of amusement. "Why are men such idiots?"

Sara giggles, fingers tightening again. "Because they do things like cheese rolling and ice football."

My mouth hitches up.

Mandy softens further, moving next to me, slinging an arm around my shoulders. "And soccer with bowling balls like that TikTok you sent me?"

"Exactly," Sara says.

I laugh.

Mandy squeezes me. "That's better, honey." A beat. "In fact," she says. "*All* of this sounds better."

"I don't know everything that's going on with him," I admit with a sigh. "But...I know it's something. And I know it has to be something big, something he's almost ready to tell me."

"Yeah?" Sara asks.

"He was going to tell me," I say then bite my lip. "I just..." A wince. "We keep getting distracted."

Mandy snorts.

Sara grins. Then sobers. "Distracted," she agrees softly. "But also...sometimes it's easier to avoid something you know is going to hurt."

I mock scowl. "How the fuck did you get into my head?"

She bumps her shoulder with mine. "I've harnessed my Brit Mind Reading Powers."

I nudge her back, heart a little less heavy. "Truthfully, I've been going around and around with this in my brain—thinking about all the mistakes I've made, hating Stefan for what he did, hurting because we've missed out on so much and put Rox through the wringer and—" I exhale. "I guess it's nice to get it out of my own head."

"So," Mandy teases, "just to be clear, you're thanking us for being nosy bitches?"

"I don't believe I used those *exact* words," I grumble. "But I do appreciate it."

Mandy laughs, squeezes me again then drops her arm. "So, what are you going to do?"

"What I should have from the beginning," I say.

She lifts her brows.

"Fight for him."

THIRTY-THREE

STEFAN

I'm sitting in the kitchen with a beer, waiting for my woman to walk in the door.

My. Woman.

Something I promised myself I wouldn't think over the last year.

And yet, I'm right back here anyway.

Sitting in this stool, waiting for the sound of the garage door to rumble open, for Brit to come in through the mudroom, to walk down the hall and appear in the kitchen.

Stupid.

But...

I fucking can't.

I was delusional to think it might even be possible to keep away from her.

It's like living without the other half of my soul.

I was trying to protect her—but instead I hurt her.

So now, no matter the hour, no matter the outcome, no matter that every instinct in me is saying to avoid this conversation, to retreat, to protect her from the truth...

I *have* to tell her everything.

I saw her on the ice, saw her face when she was watching Dan and Rox, the yearning and pain—and not from making a killer play between the pipes.

And it wasn't pain *I'd* caused for once.

It was the pain one feels when they know a chapter of their life is coming to a close.

I know.

Because I was there not all that long ago.

Because she helped me see it through, to find who I was on the other side, and—

I'm going to do the same for her.

I'm going to be around.

Even if—

The fear that slides through me is so intense, so agonizing, so like what sent me out the door in the first place that I have to clench my teeth, grip the edge of the counter, barely resisting the urge to run again.

"That good, huh?" Dan mutters.

I jump, not having heard the sneaky fucker come in behind me.

I inhale slowly, exhale silently.

"I'm good," I mutter.

"You sure about that?"

"Yup." I take a long sip of my beer.

"You know what I do."

Know that he can murder me, make my body disappear, and then make the world forget I existed at all?

Yeah, I know that.

"I didn't want to hurt your sister, Dan," I mutter, then drain the bottle and set it on the counter with a soft *clink*.

"You just felt like you had to?"

"I—"

Well, yeah.

But even I can see what a fucking cop-out of an answer that sounds like.

Dan sighs, moves to the fridge, pulling out two more bottles of beer and popping their tops. He hands one to me, takes a sip of his. Then sighs, leaning his hip against the counter. "You know what I do," he says again.

"Yeah, I know that you could unalive me, Dan," I mutter, tracing the label on the bottle with my thumb. "I know that you'll do it if I hurt her again."

"You *know* what I do," he repeats a third time.

I sigh, irritated now. "*Yes*," I snap. "I know what you do, Dan."

"So, you know I have access to things," he says. "Things other people might not."

I narrow my eyes.

"Things like medical records."

I freeze, then panic snakes down my spine again. *Fuck.* I open my mouth—

And the garage door rumbles open.

My head whips toward the hall, listening to the engine of Brit's car echoing through the garage, hearing it shut off a moment later, knowing that I have seconds to put this shit to rest. "Don't you—"

Which is the exact moment I hear her cry out, a barely audible yell through the walls, through the door.

I'm up on my feet in an instant, dropping the bottle onto the counter, not giving a fuck when it topples over, sending beer pouring off the granite.

I haul ass out of the kitchen, down the hall, through the mudroom, and into the garage, distantly aware of Dan following me, but I skid to a stop the moment I pass through, thrown for a second before I process the scene in front of me.

Then I do.

Process it, that is.

Process Brit pressed back against her closed driver's side door, arm outstretched, keeping a man at a distance.

No.

Not a man.

Trey.

What the *actual* fuck?

But I don't stop to process *that*, not at fucking all. I'm moving again, sprinting over to her, shoving my body between hers and Trey's, forcing the asshole back. "What the fuck are you doing?" I growl.

For one second, he seems confused.

And then that turns to anger. "What the fuck do you think *you're* doing, asshole?" he snaps.

"I'm not the one assaulting Brit in her garage."

"No," he says, eyes flaring with a special brand of crazy that I really don't like. "You're the one who divorced her."

Well technically, I filed the papers.

But the divorce isn't final.

Thank fuck.

"Just go, Trey," Brit says softly.

"But I—"

She sighs. "I told you when you came to the rink last week—"

I stiffen, head whipping around and sending a sudden wave of dizziness through me, but I push that down, lift my brows.

She winces but doesn't acknowledge my unspoken questions —namely, why the fuck she didn't mention that little tidbit sooner. "It wouldn't work out between us," she tells Trey firmly. "Even *if* Stefan and I weren't back together."

Trey rocks back as though those words are a physical blow. "But—"

"I believe she's made it clear that she doesn't want anything to do with you," I grit out, a throb beginning in my temple. "So, get the fuck out and don't you ever touch her or approach her again."

"Want to tell me who the fuck is this?"

Dan's icy cold voice has us all freezing.

I feel Brit's lungs expand from where she's pressed to my back, but I don't give her a chance to answer. Mostly because that throb in my temple has expanded, is turning into a full-blown headache, but also partly because I don't actually want Dan to have to commit murder and disappear a body on our account.

"No one important," I say. "Trey is just leaving."

"What's Trey's last name?" Dan asks silkily.

"It doesn't matter—" Brit prevaricates, clearly picking up on the note of murder in the air.

But the dumbass doesn't recognize the sudden danger he's in. Because he turns and looks at Dan. "Martinez."

I watch Dan make a mental note of that. "Birth date?" he asks just as smoothly.

"March 12th—" Trey, the moron, freezes. "Wait— why do you want to know my birth date?"

"You should go," Dan says.

He scowls. "Not until I talk to Brit. I need—"

"Look asshole," I mutter, head positively throbbing now. "You need to get the fuck out of here. It's the middle of the night. Brit's made it clear she doesn't want anything to do with you."

"I didn't mean to scare her," Trey says dumbly.

"Which time?" she mutters.

Trey narrows his eyes. "You wanted me to kiss you, and—"

Brit settles her hand on my shoulder, pushes me slightly forward, just enough so that she can slip out from behind me.

But when she goes to step toward Dipshit McGee, I wind my arm around her waist, draw her back against me. "No," I mutter, head starting to spin.

She stills, just for a second.

Then her hand settles on my arm. But she doesn't fight my hold, doesn't stop me from keeping her close, just rests back against me and turns her gaze to address Trey. "You hurt me."

I feel Dan move closer, body taut and ready to strike.

"I don't think you meant to," she says. "But you slammed me

down into the rocks and left my mouth bleeding, and"—a breath —"and I told you no."

Dan jerks and finally the idiot in front of me seems to realize the danger he's in because he looks to the side, pales, and staggers back a step. "I should—" He hitches a thumb over his shoulder.

"Yes," I grit out, stomach churning, nausea spreading, bile rising up in the back of my throat. I tighten my grip on Brit, spread my legs a bit further apart, bracing myself against the dizziness that's sweeping up and threatening to send me to the concrete floor.

Dammit.

I haven't felt like this since the first time, since right before...I decided on a divorce.

Brit tugs lightly at my arm and I feel that dizziness increase, have to lean back against the car, have to release her so I don't take us both down to the concrete floor, legs braced or not.

Fucking stupid.

Fucking—

I waver, bump into the mirror, folding it back against the car.

"Stefan," Brit begins, turning toward me, concern lining her face. "Are you all right?"

"I—" I shake my head, trying to dislodge the black creeping in. "I'm fine," I lie. "I'm just tired and need—"

But the black edging into my vision won't go away.

The black is increasing, is growing and taking over and—

It's all I see.

Thirty-Four

BRIT

One second, Stefan is holding me tightly against his big, strong frame.

The next that arm is slipping free and he's collapsing back against my car.

I hear the *thunk* and turn to face him, seeing that he's gone a ghastly shade of gray. His eyes roll back—

And then he collapses.

I grab for him, distantly aware of my brother moving toward Stefan to do the same.

But neither of us are fast enough.

Stefan collapses, body hitting the concrete hard, head slamming back against the car.

"Shit," Dan mutters, skidding to a halt, dropping to his knees. "Easy," he says, slipping his hand behind Stefan's head, gently shifting his body, laying him out on the floor when he tries to get up. "Just give yourself a second."

"I'm fine," Stefan snaps, tucking his elbows beneath him and trying to sit up.

Only his face goes gray again and he starts to collapse.

"Christ," Dan says, plunking a hand on his shoulder, pushing him back down. "Just...stay." His eyes come to mine. "Be right back."

And then he's walking out of the garage, disappearing around the corner. It takes me a second, but then I realize he's checking for Trey.

Because he's not in the garage.

And also...what the fuck had he been thinking coming into my garage in the first place?

And...how did he get through the gate?

And—

I exhale.

It doesn't matter. I'll take it up with security—or maybe I'll just sic Pascal on him. Or—

Right.

This is probably not the time to be thinking about security or Trey or Pascal and his super sneaking skills that rival Dan's. This would be the time to focus on the fact that my husband is currently white as a sheet and sprawled out on the garage floor.

Because he collapsed.

He shivers, a full-body one that I feel as he's pressed against my thigh. "What's going on, honey?" I ask softly, gently touching a pale and sweaty cheek.

"I—"

"He's gone," Dan says, moving into the garage, walking past us, and hitting the button to close the door. As it rumbles shut, he comes back. "Ready?" he asks, but I don't get a chance to respond because he's not talking to me. He's crouching next to Stefan, slipping an arm around Stefan's shoulders, and pushing him up to sitting.

And then he's all but hauling my husband to his feet and pausing.

Waiting as Stefan wavers.

Repositioning his arm so that Stefan can lean more heavily against him.

"Breathe," he orders.

Stefan nods.

Does just that.

I open my mouth. Close it.

Know that whatever questions I have, whatever concerns are rattling around in my head, whatever worries are tearing at my heart...

They're not a priority.

We need to get Stefan inside.

Then I can put the rest of the pieces together.

I shift around the men, moving in front of them and hustling up the three stairs that lead into the house so I can push open the door, can hold it wide as Dan helps Stefan maneuver inside.

I close and lock it, start to follow them down the hall.

"Shoes," Stefan murmurs.

"What?" Dan asks.

"Brit always takes off her shoes, hangs up her hoodie and bag," he mumbles. "She should do that. My shit shouldn't stop her from doing what she needs to."

I still, sucking in a rapid breath.

What the fuck?

But because it seems to matter to him, I pause and toe off my shoes, hang up my bag, my hoodie, and then I follow my brother and husband down the hall.

I follow them through the kitchen, my heart squeezing when I see that my snack is sitting on the kitchen island—a plate with veggies and hummus, a chocolate milk.

Taking care of me.

Like he used to.

I exhale quietly, eyes stinging, then turn and follow him and Dan slowly up the stairs, down the hall. Into my—*our*—bedroom. I slip by them when they pause just inside the doorway so I can pull back the blankets, shift around the pillows.

Then Dan's there, helping Stefan sit on the edge of the mattress.

I move close, lift Stefan's feet, settling him back against the pillows, tugging the blanket up and over him. "Your color looks better," I murmur.

He forces a smile. "I'm fine. Go have your snack." He nods toward the open door.

Winces.

"What?" I ask, taking his hand.

"Nothing," he mutters. "I've just got a headache. I'm good." He forces a smile. "I promise."

I'd believe him.

Except, he's fucking lying.

And not even doing it well with that gray-ass skin and rubbing at his temple.

I squeeze his hand, hold his pale blue eyes for a couple of heartbeats, seeing the pain in the deepening creases surrounding them. "I'll go get you something for your headache."

"I'm fine."

I squeeze again, say more firmly. "I'll go get you something."

He forces a smile. "Thanks, sweetheart."

My gaze drags across Dan's as I leave the room, and then I'm hurrying down the stairs, moving into the kitchen, getting him a glass of water, snagging the bottle of Tylenol from the cabinet. I tuck the latter under my arm, snag my snack and chocolate milk —because I know he won't let it go, and I'd rather eat my snack in bed beside him than continue arguing with him about it.

Then I carry everything upstairs, footsteps silent on the carpet as I move down the hall.

But their voices, softly echoing out into the hallway, aren't.

"That's none of your business." Stefan's tone is weary, exhausted, and I slide to a stop, heart suddenly in my throat.

"Enough fucking excuses," my brother says. "You need to tell her." A beat. "Or I will."

"She's had a hard enough time lately without dealing with her husband having—"

I drop the plate, the glass of water, the milk, making a giant mess on the carpet.

But I barely register it.

Because the rest of Stefan's sentence is echoing through my mind.

And I can't process it.

Because I couldn't have possibly heard *that*.

I didn't fucking hear that.

I *couldn't* have.

Dan's head is suddenly poking out through the doorway, expression stark.

But I can't process *that* either, can't process that he knew and didn't tell me, can't process that the secret the man I love kept from me was this big.

This devastating.

I push past my brother, rush over to the bed, to my husband who's—

A fucking liar.

"You have fucking cancer?" I blurt.

Thirty-Five

Stefan

"*You have fucking cancer?*"

I freeze, know that horror's written all over my face, because I see the same in Dan's as we look from each other...to Brit, now standing next to the bed.

And she's...

Devastated.

Tears filling her eyes, obscuring the chocolate-brown irises. "Please tell me I'm having some sort of delusion," she says. "Please tell me that I didn't fucking hear that you have cancer."

"Brit," I begin, sitting up, swinging my legs over the edge of the mattress, hating the way the fatigue claws at me. I mostly feel fine with all of this shit, normal except for the lump in my balls, the slight soreness. But it's the tiredness that is the worst.

Pervasive, comes on without warning.

And then I can be fine for days, for weeks, for so long it seems like I made it all up.

Only...

I remember the same with my mom, how it would take her down without warning, lay her flat for days and days and *days*.

"What kind?"

"Testicular," I whisper.

The air in the room grows taut before she inhales, holds it for a long moment before exhaling in a sharp hiss. Then she murmurs, "Testicular cancer."

I nod.

Her eyes close, and I know what she's thinking. That I've always wanted to have more kids, that we've been waiting until she's retired to have them.

And that future might have been stolen from us.

Because of me.

"I banked my sperm," I tell her quickly. "I should be able to have kids once I'm recovered, but just in case that can't happen, we'll be fine—"

Silence again.

Hurt and silence and guilt and—

I am a fucking idiot.

I push the rest of the way up from the mattress, take a step toward her, hating when she skitters back. "It'll be okay," I tell her. "I've got it figured out. I promise. I know it was stupid to hide this, to separate when I should have told you, but—" I grind my teeth together, push on. "I wasn't thinking clearly and—"

"You weren't thinking clearly." Neutral words.

Deadly words.

"I wasn't," I agree. "I was a fucking idiot, but look, I've made the arrangements. I've already delayed my treatment. I'll wait for chemo until the season's over, and then when the rough stuff hits, it won't impact the team—"

Her entire body jerks. *"What?"*

"When things are calmer," I go on. "I'll get this shit taken care of like last time, and the doctor is going to make sure it doesn't come back. This round, he's going to be more aggressive."

Another jerk. "*This* round?"

I blather on, "It won't take long, and I'll feel good enough when preseason comes around and you're traveling again that I can cover Rox. Though, we have Tiff too, so we'll be extra covered and you won't need to worry..." I trail off because it feels like all of the air has been sucked out of the room.

And I realize her expression has changed, horror replacing anger as it ripples across the lines of her face.

"Last time?" she whispers, pushing against the circle of my arms. "*This* round?"

"Brit," Dan says softly, reaching for her, pulling her back against him, and hell, I'd forgotten he was even in the room. "Just take a breath," he tells her, but his face is stark, eyes telling me that for all he does know, he didn't know this.

Didn't know this was the *second* time.

I open my mouth.

But what can I possibly say?

I know I'm fucked up.

I know *I* fucked up.

I just don't know how to make this right.

She pulls away from her brother and walks toward the shelves, dropping her hands on top, hanging her head, whispering, "That's why you asked for the divorce."

"I couldn't put you through that, baby," I whisper back, taking another step toward her—slowly, carefully. "Not when you're—"

"What?" she says, whipping around. "I'm what?"

I inhale, brace, and move closer, taking her hands in mine. "It'll be okay, baby."

She tugs, but I hold fast. "How will this possibly be okay?"

"It's not serious," I say. "Not like my mom had."

Her eyes go wide, new worry creeping into the edges of her expression.

"It's treatable," I say in a hurry. "Just a few rounds of chemo, some radiation. It worked before, and—"

"It came back," she says.

Guilt ripples through me.

"Brit—" I begin.

She shakes her head. "You say it's not serious."

"It's not."

"But it came back," she whispers.

I squeeze her hands. "The doctor's going to be more aggressive this time."

Her brows furrow. "But you said you're delaying treatment."

"I—" *Damn.* I exhale silently, gently touch her cheek. "It'll be okay."

She shakes her head again, sending her ponytail flying behind her. "You're not doing this."

"Baby—"

"You're not fucking doing it!" she snaps, jerking free of my hold. "In fact, you're calling the doctor's office right fucking now and getting on the schedule immediately."

"It's not that simple, sweetheart," I begin.

"It *is* that fucking simple," she snaps, beautiful in her fury. "You pick up the phone, you make a call. You treat the fucking cancer that's growing in your body as we speak." She stomps across the room, grabs my cell from the nightstand, unlocking the screen and shoving it in my direction. "You make that call right fucking now—"

"Brit—" Dan begins, moving toward her, reaching for the phone. "Maybe you should just take a beat and—"

She jerks away from him, shoves my cell in my direction again. "Not now," she snaps at her brother before turning back to me, her rage a beauty to behold. "Make the fucking call, Stefan."

"Brit," Dan says again, carefully approaching her like she's a scared and cornered animal—and I suppose she is. Scared and cornered and hurt.

Because I fucked up.

"Babe," he says, carefully touching her shoulder. "Stefan can't get a hold of the doctor in the middle of the night."

"I—" She freezes. "I—" A shake of her head, seeming to jar herself back into focus before determination fills her frame and she shoves my phone at me a third time. "Maybe not," she says. "But you can leave a message."

Still, taut air.

Fury and hurt.

Guilt and fuck-ups.

But since I can do at least that—can make one fucking phone call—I take it from her and pull up the contact for the doctor's office.

Both of the Plantains watch as I hit the button to call, as I listen to it ring and ring, as I leave a message and ask for the office to call me back as soon as possible.

Then I hang up.

Turn back to Brit.

"I fucked up."

She jerks, voice breaking. "Yes, you did."

And then she's collapsing.

I move toward her, catching her before she can hit the floor.

Her sobs are...

Terrible.

Worse than hearing my diagnosis from the doctor.

Worse than watching my daughter get wheeled into surgery.

Worse than worrying I was going to lose my mom.

Because...

This is the woman I love.

And...*I* did this.

The door closes with a quiet *click* and I look up to see that Dan's finally left.

That it's just Brit and me.

It's just me and the woman I hurt.

It's just me and this hell that I put her through.

It's just me and—

She shoves out of my arms, jumps to her feet. "You have cancer," she says, thrusting a hand through her hair, sending her ponytail scattering, fingers clenching at the locks. "You have cancer and you lied to me."

"I..."

But I peter out.

Because...

She's not wrong.

"All these months of blaming myself," she whispers, turning away from me. "All this time—" A shake of her head. "*Tiffany.*"

"She wasn't anything more than a friend, than the woman who was looking after Roxie," I say. "You know she wasn't—"

Brit turns back. "I know."

I inhale. "I love you," I say, reaching for her. "I've always loved you. There's never been another woman, not since I saw you in the parking lot all those years ago."

She steps out of reach, shakes her head. "Maybe," she says. "But—" A sweep of her arm. "What do I do with that?"

My stomach clenches. "I know I messed up, baby. I wasn't thinking clearly. Everything that happened with my mom after her diagnosis, how sick she was, how tough the recovery was. I... just went a little crazy. All I could think about was putting you and Rox through that, and I..." I shove a hand through my hair. "I just couldn't."

"You couldn't put *me* through that."

I shake my head. "I couldn't, baby. I knew I could get it taken care of without either of you knowing, just like I know I can make this right. It's why I didn't fight you for the houses or the money. I was trying to make it as easy as possible so that when the cancer was gone for good, we could—"

She's turned into a statue.

So fucking still that one little push would send her toppling over, shattering into pieces.

Then she speaks, the words so quiet that I can barely make them out. "We could what?"

I—

Fuck.

"Baby—"

"We could what, Stefan?" she asks, stepping further away from me. "After the cancer was gone, we could what?"

I close my eyes.

And apparently that's answer enough.

"Work," she murmurs. "The team. Thinking I failed in our marriage. Worried about what kind of woman, what kind of wife I was." She sighs, fisting her hands at her sides. "Roxie having to go between two houses. And through all of that, you never stopped—" She drops her head back, exhales. "Through all of that, you never stopped to think that you could just *fucking talk to me?!*"

THIRTY-SIX

BRIT

I'm shaking.

Actually fucking *shaking*.

But I don't know if I want to curl up in a ball and start crying again or if I'm so fucking pissed that I want to throttle a man with cancer.

"What was the point of it all?" I whisper.

"The point of what?" he asks.

I just lift my brows.

His big, broad chest expands and then he's rubbing at his temples, pacing away.

I wait for an answer, but inside I'm dying a little more as each second passes, as the silence grows.

Because...I love this man.

But I don't know how to come back from it.

From *this*.

"I was trying to spare you the terror of it," he finally says, voice so soft I can barely hear it. "I remember what it was like with my mom, how the worry for her stole the air from my lungs and made it nearly impossible for me to focus, to play clearly. How I didn't want to be on the ice in case she needed me and I wouldn't be available. Worrying every time I got off that I'd have a call waiting telling me something terrible had happened. I couldn't risk that for you because...baby"—he comes close, touches my jaw —"you don't have that many seasons left. I didn't want to steal that from you."

My heart pulses—but I can't tell if it's from pain, or because part of me understands exactly what it's like to want to protect the people I love from anything.

Even if it means hurting them—

No.

I would never do what Stefan did.

Fucking *never.*

Because all it shows is that he doesn't trust me.

"So...you lied."

Regret slides across his face, buries itself deep into his eyes. "I didn't want to."

He didn't want to.

But he did anyway.

"I was supposed to be the most important person in your life," I say. "Your partner. Your rock as much as you're mine." I thump my hand against my chest. "I was supposed to be your person—the one you can tell everything and anything to, and—"

My heart squeezes hard.

And *that*, I think, is the worst part—aside from the fact that the man I love, the man I've never stopped loving has cancer, might die, that Rox might miss out on so much if that happens—

My lungs hitch.

I slam my eyes shut, just breathe.

I think aside from him suffering alone, from being sick, the worst part of all of this is that he kept something this big, this important from me.

We're supposed to be a team.

And...

He didn't trust me enough to tell me.

My nails bite hard into my palms, and I know I'm breathing too fast. My head is spinning, my heart is hurting, my body feels like a fragile piece of plaster, one soft touch will break right through it.

Tiff saying she met him at a cancer support group.

Diane giving me looks I felt I should be able to interpret—when Stefan's mother herself had fought her own cancer battle.

And Stefan—

My beautiful, gorgeous man who'd promised to always be there for me, who told me I was brighter in his eyes than the very stars shining in the sky...

He'd left me.

I knew it was wrong, that it didn't make sense, but I was too dumb to realize that the *only* reason he would have left was because of something he thought was so catastrophic, something that was so devastating that he wouldn't be thinking straight...

Something that made him feel as though he had no choice *but* to leave.

Stubborn man.

Beautiful, *stubborn* man.

Who loves me and thought that the only way to protect me...

Was to leave me.

Not talk to me.

Not trust me.

But...

Leave me.

Divorce me.

Hurt me.

"I need to go," I whisper. "I need to—"

He catches my arm when I turn away, when I start for the door, drawing me against him. "No," I say and shove lightly at his shoulders, but not hard because, God, *I* can't bear to hurt him.

Even after all of this, I can't bear to hurt him.

"I need to go," I say again.

"Brit, baby. Take a breath," he pleads. "We can talk—"

"I *need* to go."

"I made a mistake," he says. "I see that now."

"A mistake." I laugh, but it's not filled with humor, not in the fucking least.

"Sweetheart—"

"I need to fucking *go*," I pull myself free, back toward the door. "I really need to go."

He takes my arm, draws me against him. "Baby—"

It's too much—the scent of him surrounding me, the warmth of his body, the sense of *rightness* each and every time his skin comes in contact with mine.

Because it *is* right.

And it's wrong.

All of this is wrong.

I jerk away from him, spin toward the door.

"Don't go," he says as I reach for the handle.

That drags through me like a dull blade—jagged and painful and brutally—and my fingers convulse on the doorknob, spasming against the cold metal.

I clamp my eyes closed.

A tear slips free anyway, sliding down my cheek, dripping off my jaw.

But when I feel him coming closer, the force holding me in place disappears.

I wrench at the knob, pull the wooden panel wide. Dan—as expected—is standing at the end of the hall, a silent sentry who sees right through any semblance of the mask I manage to erect.

My footsteps falter.

And then he's there, tucking an arm around my shoulders, but when he starts to guide me down the hall, I see the stained carpet.

He's cleaned up the glass I dropped, the remnants of my snack.

But the damage has been done.

On my carpet.

On me.

I pull away from him.

"Brit," he begins.

"You knew," I say, tone sharp, but quiet. I can't wake Rox right now. I fucking *can't*. "You knew and didn't tell me."

"I only just found out—"

"When?" I ask.

The guilt sliding across his face is enough of an answer.

"Right," I whisper.

He knew.

And he kept it from me.

That's...another hurt.

And it's one too many.

"Don't," I say when he comes toward me. "Just *don't*."

"Baby—"

I look down the hall, see Stefan coming toward me.

"—just take a second and—"

I can't.

Do this.

See him.

Talk to either of them.

But I'm not a coward, despite my idiocy of the last months. I don't run or cower. I face the puck, cut off the angles, protect the crease.

Protect...

Myself.

I inhale, hold my breath for a long moment, and then I exhale, look at both of them. "I need some space," I say.

Dan's mouth presses flat.

Stefan takes a step toward me.

"From both of you." I grind my teeth together. "Please respect that."

Then I whirl on my heel and get the fuck out of this house.

Thirty-Seven

Stefan

I know letting her walk away is the biggest mistake I can make. Or the second biggest considering the rest of my fucking idiocy in keeping up with this sham.

But...she's asked for time.

And how can I deny her that?

Dan must have the same thought because he stays in place too as Brit turns and all but runs away. I listen to the sound of her footsteps on the stairs, across the kitchen, the slam of the door out to the garage shutting behind her. The rumble of the wide metal door opening and her car's engine starting up.

A rumble that fades as she drives away.

Fuck.

I thrust my hand through my hair, clenching at the strands, wanting to rip them from my scalp.

I just let her go.

Again.

Dan sighs, shakes his head. "I'll give her some time to cool down and go after her."

"No," I mutter. "*I'll* go after her."

Brit's brother turns and shakes his head. "Haven't you done enough?"

I grit my teeth. "I didn't want to hurt her."

"What did you expect?" he snaps, tossing up his hands. "How the fuck did you expect her to react when she found out you kept something this big from her?"

"I promised," I say. "I promised I'd never get between her and her career. What do you think she would do the moment she found out I have cancer? She'd be here. Not with the team. Not on the ice. And she doesn't have all that much time left to play and—"

Dan is suddenly in my face, hand gripping the collar of my shirt, big body shaking with fury. "Do you think she would honestly choose hockey over the man she loves?"

I drop my hand on top of his. "No." I peel his fingers back, release my shirt from his grip. "I *know* she'd pick me," I say. "And that's why I couldn't let her."

His eyes blaze with fury.

Fury that fades as he slowly drops his hand to his side. "You're a fucking idiot," he mutters.

"Yeah," I agree. "But I'm an idiot who loves your sister enough to do whatever I can to protect her. I'll make it up to her. I swear I will."

When I'm better and she finishes out her career, she'll see.

She'll understand.

I'm giving her a gift.

"Maybe," he says, turning and heading for the guest room, "but have you considered how much that *protection* has hurt her?"

I open my mouth to reply, but he doesn't give me a chance.

The door to the spare bedroom *clicks* closed.

And I stand there for a good long while, waiting for something, anything to happen—Brit to come home, Rox to wake up, Dan to emerge from the guest room telling me that he'll help me figure out how to make this right.

But nothing does.

It's just me in an empty hallway.

Just me alone.

Like it's been from the moment the doctor first told me I had cancer.

I've gotten used to it—or convinced myself I had anyway.

But right now, staring into the darkness, after losing Brit again, it's too much.

I turn around, walk down the hall, and lay in bed.

For a long, long time.

But eventually that solitude gets to me, and I give up on my bed, on waiting, hoping, praying to the universe that Brit will come home.

I toss back the blankets, slip into Roxie's room.

And it's there that I'm finally able to fall asleep.

To the sound of my daughter's slow and even breathing.

———

"Daddy's sleeping," I hear my daughter whisper.

Which means she's all but yelling.

"Well then," my mom says. "Let's not wake him up."

I groan and roll my head from side to side, trying to ease the ache that comes from being too fucking old and deciding it was a good idea to sleep on my daughter's floor.

"Too late," I hear my dad say dryly as I rub a hand over my face and manage to peel open my eyes. "Mom, Dad, what are you guys doing here?"

"We're supposed to go out to brunch with you, Brit, Dan, and Roxie," my mom says. "And Tiff is going to meet us at Molly's before she has to go study for her midterm, remember?"

No, I don't remember.

Because I was doing my personal best to be a fucking idiot.

"Did Brit get in terribly late?" she asks. "We can always bring her something back if she needs to sleep in..."

I try to bite back my wince but clearly don't do a good enough job because I see my dad's gaze sharpen, my mom's eyes widen. "What happened?" she asks, but I cut my eyes toward Rox, who's tugging on her fluffy rainbow-colored unicorn boots—complete with a mane and horn in the corner of the room.

She understands my look and doesn't press.

"Why don't you go find Uncle Dan?" I tell her when she runs back over to me and launches herself into my lap. "That way, we can get breakfast."

"'Kay," she murmurs, throwing her arms around me for a quick, tight hug, and then she's running from the room, yelling, "Uncle Danny!"

"What is it?" my mom says the moment she leaves the room.

I want to lie.

But I've been doing entirely too much of that as of late.

"Brit found out about the cancer."

My dad's lungs inflate in a hiss of air.

My mom grimaces and reaches out to take my hand. "Did she react very poorly?"

My dad—who hadn't agreed with keeping this secret from the beginning—snorts. "What do you think, Diane?"

She swats at him. "Not now, Pierre," she says. "Of course she didn't take it well. Brit has to be hurt and"—she pushes up to her feet—"I should talk to her, help her understand—"

"She's not here," I tell her. "She asked for space, and since I've spent the last year doing what *I* wanted to do"—or what I felt as though I *had* to do—"I'm giving her what she asked me for."

My mom nibbles at her bottom lip. "But—"

"Mom," I say. "I owe her this much."

She sucks in a breath. "Yeah, baby," she says, cupping my jaw lightly in her hand. "I think you do." A beat before she turns for the door, my dad trailing her. "Get changed and let's feed the beasts. And we'll buy some extra pastries for Brit."

I crawl to my feet, start to follow them.

Which is why I see her mouth quirk up as she glances back over her shoulder.

"Because if there's anything that gets through to a woman's heart, it's pastries."

THIRTY-EIGHT

BRIT

"I knew you'd be here."

I still, fingers clenching on the concrete wall that overlooks the ocean.

The sun is bright overhead, breaking through San Francisco's typical shroud of fog and shining off the pools of water that abut the beach not all that far in front of me.

"It's better at sunset," I tell Diane as she sits next to me, taking in the splendor of the Sutro Baths, an old ruin of saltwater pools that were never as successful as their owner hoped they would be. Now, all that's left is the foundation of the old bath house and pools of algae-covered water.

But it makes for a great place to sit and stare out at the ocean —the cluster of jutting rocks in the distance, the waves crashing against the shore.

I'm not alone, but there are so few people here at the moment that I might as well be.

Except, of course, for my mother-in-law, who's decided to invade my peace.

But even as the resentful words cross my mind, they're immediately pushed away.

Because I love Diane.

Because she's been one of my biggest fans, my biggest supporters from the moment she met me.

More of a mom than mine had ever been.

"You knew," I say, and it's not a question.

"His health story isn't mine to share." She bumps her shoulder against mine. "And I'd tell him the same if the roles were reversed."

"Right," I mutter, staring at the waves.

Another nudge of her shoulder against mine, and a....

I frown.

A *crinkle*.

I look down, see a brown bag printed with Molly's logo has appeared in front of my face.

"It's not a Cheat Day." But my fingers still close around the bag anyway.

"I don't think Rebecca will mind," she says. "Not after the news you had."

"Self-medicating with baked goods?" I ask dryly.

Diane's mouth curves. "Desperate times call for desperate measures."

I inhale.

But then I unroll the top of the bag, peek inside. "White chocolate and cranberry."

Diane scoots a little closer, mirroring my position. "Of course," she says. "It's your favorite." A nod of her head. "There's also an apple turnover in there."

My mouth quirks up at the edges. "Bringing out the big guns."

"Of course I am."

My smile is small, I know it is. But considering the last hours, that I've managed to smile at all is a freaking miracle.

"I thought he should tell you," she murmurs. "I want you to know that."

Something like relief blooms in my belly.

At least until she says, "But I understand why he didn't."

I glare out at the vicious ocean, its waters turbulent and frigid. "I don't," I snap. "We were married—" I shake my head.

Are married, I guess, since we haven't signed the final paperwork.

Are married since I'm not going to let my idiot of a husband fight this battle alone.

Are married because despite everything...

I love him.

"He betrayed your trust," she says when I don't go on, just narrow my eyes out at those ever-persisting waves. "He should have told you. Of course he should have."

I sigh. "But he was trying to protect me."

Her hand rests on my knee, squeezes lightly. "And in doing that he hurt you, and he undermined the relationship you have worked so hard to build over the years."

My throat goes tight, eyes stinging. "Yes," I whisper.

Her fingers squeeze again. "He should have told you," she says again. "But he didn't." A light pat before she passes me a napkin, tucking it into the pocket of my hoodie. "Now you'll have to decide what you're going to do about that."

I inhale, eyes sliding closed. "I know what I'm going to do about it," I whisper.

She's still beside me.

And quiet, nothing but the sound of the waves beating against the rocks, the other conversations around us, filling the space between us.

Patient.

Kind.

Like her son is...usually.

Like her son was so many times over the course of our relationship.

Before I came home to him sitting in the kitchen, divorce papers on the counter in front of him.

I know what I want to do—

"But I'm scared."

Her arm wraps around my shoulders. "I know, sweetheart."

I sigh.

She reaches into the bag, pulls out the cookie, and hands it to me. "Eat, baby girl. And then sit here and enjoy the view, the quiet, the space you're taking." She touches my cheek. "Sit and think about what you want, what you need, what needs to change, and then, whenever you're ready, come home."

My lids slide closed.

"Because we all love you so much, honey, but not as much as Stefan does—and he needs you."

A tear slips free. "Diane," I whisper.

Her palm cups my cheek. "Carbs. Space. And then see you soon, sweetheart."

I nod. "Okay," I whisper.

Her mouth curves. "That's my girl." And then she's pressing a kiss to my forehead before pushing up to her feet, walking away.

Leaving me to the ocean and the blue sky and the solitude that I need to get my thoughts together.

Leaving me to think.

When I already know the answers to all of the questions rattling through my mind.

THIRTY-NINE

STEFAN

"Are you living with Mom again?"

I look up from the stack of papers on the counter and see my daughter is standing in the entrance to the kitchen, expression suspicious.

Tiff glances up from where she's making cookies, her eyes connecting with mine. She wordlessly picks up the bowl, tucks it away in the fridge, and walks out of the room.

I close the folder, turn to my daughter. "Why do you ask, honey?"

"Because we haven't been back to the other house."

I open my mouth.

"And your stuff is in Mom's room."

I close it again.

"And you and Mom have been spending all your time together." A beat as she looks down at her sock-covered feet, toes flexing lightly against the hardwood floor. "Like you used to."

My throat tightens.

"Before you said you guys were getting a divorce." Her voice is quiet now and sad, enough that my heart squeezes tightly, the guilt tying my insides into knots creeps up my throat, threatens to steal the words from my tongue. "Are you going to get married again?"

Another squeeze.

Because now sad has been replaced by hope.

And, God, I have so much I've fucked up.

So much to make up for.

All because I was too much of a coward to face something hard.

I inhale, eyes sliding closed, knowing that my doctor was right —it's not me needing to take care of Roxie and Brit, not me wanting to protect them...or not completely anyway.

It's fear.

Of whom I'll become because of this illness.

Of how I will need to lean on those around me.

What it will make me if *I'm* not the one who everyone relies on.

"Dad?"

I exhale, peel open my eyes, and look at my beautiful, amazing daughter. "I need to talk to your mother about that."

Her little body is still. "So...you are?"

Dammit.

I push off my stool, move over to her, crouching in front of her and taking her hands in mine. "I don't know what's going to happen between your mom and me—"

She scowls. "That's just something grown-ups say when they don't want to answer a question."

I almost laugh.

Because she's too fucking smart for her own good.

But that's not the right response, not right now, not when this is too important.

"Rox, honey," I say. "I want to answer that question. I want to tell you that your mom and I are going to get back together and everything is going to be totally fine and that we're going to go back to the way things were before."

Her eyes slide away.

"But I really—"

"Did you fall in love with someone else?" she asks.

I blink. "What?" I shake my head. "No," I say. "Of course not. Your mom is the only woman I've ever loved."

She looks back, hope blooming across her face. "Really?"

"Yeah, baby. *Really*," I tell her. "But I messed up and I hurt her, and it's not going to be easy to make that right."

"What'd you do?"

I touch her cheek. "That's an adult topic for an adult conversation."

She scowls.

"And you can get mad or demand I tell you, but I'm not going to." I touch her cheek again. "All you need to know is that I messed up big, baby girl. I hurt your mom and I feel awful, and I'm going to find a way to make it right."

"You hurt Mom?"

The accusation in her tone slices deep.

But I'm not going to deny that this shit is my fault.

"Yeah, baby," I say.

"Why?"

That's the fucking question of the hour, isn't it?

I exhale. "Even adults make mistakes."

Her brows furrow. "Have you tried saying you're sorry?"

God, my beautiful, sweet girl. I cup her jaw. "That's a great idea, baby."

Eagerness creeps in. "Mom likes it when you say sorry."

I nod.

"And she likes presents too," she says.

"Yeah?"

Rox starts to smile. "You should buy her a Squishmallow."

My mouth ticks up. "You think Mom would like that as an apology present?"

A solemn nod. "Yup. She takes Danny Dino with her on every road game."

The other half of my mouth curves. "That's true," I agree. "So, will you help me pick out a friend for Danny?"

She tilts her head to the side. "Are you going to apologize after we get it?"

I incline my head. "I'll give her the biggest apology ever."

"And then will you make us all pizza again?"

I ruffle her hair. "You just had pizza a couple of days ago."

"So?"

"So," I say, "I think we should expand our meal choices a little bit, don't you think?"

She wrinkles her nose.

"How about we hit Target and see what looks good?" I ask, tugging at a strand of her hair. "And then we can pick out a friend for Danny *and* Mr. Fluffernut while we're there."

Her eyes light up. "Can we go right now?"

I chuckle at the enthusiastic question, but nod, knowing she's been going more than a little stir crazy not being able to do all of her normal after-school sports and activities, especially since it will still be a good while longer before her doctor-mandated rest will be over.

And she's like her mama.

She likes to be busy.

She likes to be helpful.

She likes to get shit done.

So, I don't fight it, don't point out that she's already been to brunch today and played video games with Dan all afternoon. I don't remind her that Tiff is making her cookies while on her study break (and also, because she's trying to avoid the terror known as her mother).

I just ruffle her hair again and straighten, say, "Yeah, baby girl. We can go right now."

"Yes!" She fist-pumps.

I tilt my head toward the stairs. "Go get your shoes on, and we'll head out."

"Okay, Dad!" she says and starts running from the room, and, God, if I could bottle her powers of recovery, I'd be unstoppable.

I start stacking papers, setting them to the side.

"Dad?"

I pause, look up, see that she's hesitating in the doorway. "Yeah, baby girl?"

"Does this mean I *don't* get two Christmases?"

My mouth drops open.

But I don't get a chance to answer.

Because laughter has me jerking, my gaze shooting toward the hall.

And everything in me goes absolutely still as I see Brit standing there.

Forty

Brit

"Mom!"

My heart melts as Rox sprints toward me, throwing her arms around my waist, hugging me tight.

"Hey, baby girl." I hug her back then ruffle her hair when she pulls away, starts to hustle from the kitchen.

"Dad says he messed up," she calls over her shoulder. "He's really sorry."

I still.

But she doesn't, just sprints from the room.

"Rox?" Stefan calls. "You'll only be getting one Christmas."

She pauses, wrinkles her nose. "But will I still get Tiff?"

He opens his mouth to reply, but I beat him to it. "Tiff is family," I say.

And that has Rox's expression relaxing, her lips curving, and then she's running back over to me, squeezing me tight. "Good." She looks over her shoulder at Stefan. "Can Mom come with us to Target too?"

His eyes warm. "Absolutely."

"And Tiff?"

"If she wants to."

"Yes!" A fist pump before Rox is running out of the room and tearing off down the hall. I listen to her footsteps on the stairs and then I turn to Stefan, moving to him, taking his hands in mine. "I am so fucking pissed off at you," I whisper.

His expression sobers. "I know."

"I can't believe you would put us through this, that you would lie and hide the truth."

"I know."

"And I can't believe that you wouldn't trust me to be there for you."

He touches my cheek. "I know."

"And..." I breathe for a moment then push out, "I can't believe that I just stepped aside and didn't fight for us."

His brows furrow.

"But I also can't believe that I let you push me away, that I just stepped aside and sat in my hurt and—"

"I didn't make it easy, baby. I fucking filed divorce papers, refused to talk to you."

"I allowed myself to be a victim," I tell him. "Were you wrong with what you did? Fuck yes, you were. You were wrong and stupid and I cannot believe this is something you didn't tell me. It shows you don't trust me, don't want me to be there at your side, and I don't know how we can move forward from that."

He flinches.

"But..." I sigh. "I also understand where you were coming from—watching your mom be so sick, experiencing things being precarious, almost losing her too many times. I know you were scared of that future, especially since it was all happening right around the time of the shooting and me getting hurt." I suck in a breath, release it. "And on top of all the hiccups we had as a married couple."

"Baby—"

"And I didn't do us any favors retiring and then going back to playing, too fucking terrified of who I am without hockey."

His jaw flexes and he shakes his head. "Yeah, baby, all of that is true." A breath, his voice so damned gentle, I feel it in my soul. "But who helped me with my own future when I didn't know what I wanted to do?"

I suck in a breath.

"And instead, *I* walked out, pushed you away, and—"

"You have fucking cancer," I growl, cupping his face in my hands and forcing him to hold my stare. "Of course you weren't thinking straight—"

He shakes his head. "I should have done better."

Her mouth kicks up. "I should have too."

"Brit—"

"Stefan," I say. "We both know we have work to do," I whisper. "A lot of it because you didn't tell me, but also, I stepped back when I should have fought for us."

He covers my hands with his own. "I wouldn't have let you in," he says. "Even if you had pushed harder than you did. I was too wrapped up in everything, too concerned with protecting you and Rox—" He clamps his teeth together, pulls back, a muscle in his jaw flexing.

"What?" I ask.

"That's true," he murmurs. "But it's also a lie."

I frown.

"I did—*do*—want to protect you, especially when I thought I could handle this shit and then could come back and make it right."

"But?" I ask when he doesn't go on, knowing there's more.

"I was scared."

My heart squeezes. "Yeah, honey, of course you were."

"No." He shoves a hand through his hair, exhales sharply. "I was too fucking scared and I almost made the worst mistake of my life."

I move to him, touch his jaw. "But we're back here now," I say. "We're talking. We're going to figure it out."

He shakes his head but doesn't move away. Instead, he comes closer, wraps me in his arms, and God, that feels nice. "I almost lost you. God, baby, how can I ever make it up to you?"

"We talk," I tell him. "We check in. We get some fucking therapy. And"—I pull back, stare deep into his eyes—"you listen to your doctor's advice and you get treatment so you can stick around with us for a long time."

His face gentles. "How did I ever think I could do this without you?"

Deep inside, something heals.

It's not perfect.

How can it be?

But...it's like the edges of that wound are starting to itch, preparing themselves to heal.

"We've never done anything small, have we?" I ask. "Divorce instead of talking. Winning Stanley Cups in arenas that hold twenty thousand plus people. Courtship on national TV, our relationship troubles broadcast just as wide."

He grins. Finally. And I feel that wound *start* to close. "No, baby. We've never done anything small."

"So we're going to keep doing that." I take his hand. "Living big and doing it together. No more secrets. No more hiding away. No more trying to do it on our own."

The last is said as a warning.

And he knows it.

Which is why he grins and draws me closer. "I love you, Brit Plantain."

"I love *you*, Stefan Barie."

He rests his forehead against mine, sighs. "And I know I've got work to do—with you, with Rox, with beating this fucking disease once and for all, but I promise to make this right, to make it up to you, to—"

My heart squeezes. "How about instead of trying to make it

right, to fix all the broken pieces that won't ever be the same, we move forward?" A beat. "Together."

His inhale is sharp, but then he nods, bending so that our mouths are aligned, our lips touching, and—

"Did Mom accept your apology, Dad?"

We freeze, lips barely brushing, and then I start laughing.

And, best of all, so does he. And Rox. And Tiff when she ventures back into the kitchen.

And then...

We all pull it together and go buy Squishmallows.

Because everyone knows about the healing properties of stuffed animals.

EPILOGUE

The buzzer has gone.

The game is over.

But I'm getting back onto the ice as usual.

It's a comfortable place, has always been one of my favorite places.

But it's not my *only* place.

"You played great, baby."

I turn, see Stefan standing in the hall, his skin a little pale, body a little thin, but...okay. He's just finished his treatment, and tonight, the team ran a fundraiser for the charity Stefan and I started that supports local cancer patients.

"Did you want to go home?" I say, tilting my head back down the corridor. "I'll just zip through the stuff I need to with Frankie, and—"

"I'll stay."

I bite my bottom lip. "It's late, honey."

"I'm okay."

"But you've had a long day and—"

"I feel like celebrating." He pushes off the wall. "I'm done with this shit, and"—he winds his hand into my hair, gently tilts my head up, lightly brushes his lips over mine—"my woman played her ass off tonight. So, you're going to do what you need to do"—another brush—"and then we're going to get ice cream and stay out all night celebrating like teenagers."

I still, heart pounding in my chest. "What about Rox?"

"Tiff took her home," he says and then gives me a smile—his smile. The one that never fails to make my heart skip a beat. The one that always makes me feel like I'm home.

From the first time I saw it in the parking lot of this very arena.

To right now, standing close, the cool air of the rink clinging to my cheeks.

"Okay, then," I say, running my fingers over the stubble of his beard. "Pucks. Workout. Shower." My mouth quirks. "And then ice cream."

A tug of my hair. "You've got a deal."

I laugh. "It was your idea."

Another tug. Another sexy smile. "I know. That's why I like it. Now"—he tilts his head toward the ice, toward Frankie, who's standing at the blue line with a bucket of pucks in front of him—"go and work on that glove hand."

"Rude," I say, laughter bubbling up inside of me.

But I listen to the order, and I step out onto the ice, skate toward Frankie who nods at me. "Ready, kid?" he asks, dumping over the bucket of pucks, using his stick to send them scattering in all directions.

"I'm ready," I tell him.

But I don't skate to the crease, not until he looks up and meets my eyes.

"I'm *ready*," I say again.

He stills, a puck just in front of his stick, and looks at me, *really* looks at me for a long moment, seeming to study the very depths of my soul.

And then his mouth quirks up, and he sends the puck shooting off to the side.

"Well, then, kiddo, I cannot wait for you to put the rest of us coaches to shame."

———

TIFF

"Your total is $23.26," the cashier says, tapping on the register's keyboard, the computer screen above it changing as rapidly as her fingers move.

Clickity-click. Clickity-click. Clickity-click.

She pauses, glances up.

But not at me.

At the man she's currently checking out, the man just in front of me. The man who reacts after a brief moment, jerking as though jarred from his thoughts and reaching into his pocket.

He's wearing a pair of jeans stained with so much dirt that I pity his washing machine, and his tee isn't much better, filthy and sweat-covered, plastered against a broad, well-muscled chest.

His forearms and hands are stained with something dark.

Clearly coming from some sort of hard, physical work, and on a day like today, summer clinging to the edges of a sunny spring afternoon, I envy him.

Not that I don't love my job—I'm a nanny, and my charge is awesome, and I love that it gives me the freedom to pursue my degree.

But sometimes I wouldn't mind playing hooky and getting out on one of the many trails around us on this side of the Bay, all rolling green hills and old-growth oaks and spring wildflowers.

"Sir?"

I blink, realize that while I've been daydreaming about poppies and blue lupines, the man in front of me has been searching his pockets.

And coming up empty.

"Your total is $23.26," the cashier repeats, a little sharper now.

"Right," the man says, patting his pockets in turn. "Just give me a second. I know my wallet—"

"If you can't pay, I'm going to have to ask you step aside and let the others behind you have their turn." Her tone is brusque and cold and—

Filled with disdain.

It slices through me, even though it's not directed *at* me.

Because I've lived that life.

Because even today, I calculated my own spread on the conveyor belt, sitting behind the plastic divider, to a precise degree. I know that I have exactly the amount in my account to cover my food for the week.

Food and tuition. Medical debts and gas.

All of my expenses carefully worked out.

The man keeps searching. "I know I have—"

Someone sighs behind me—a sharp irritated sound that zips through the air, stinging as it flies by me.

The man looks up, mid pocket-pat, and I almost gasp at the startling blue of his eyes.

They're as bright as the cloudless sky outside the store and filled with embarrassment that has my heart squeezing.

"If you'll just give me a moment," he murmurs, eyes narrowing as they drift behind me, presumably toward the impatient sigher and the line that's growing by the moment. "I have—"

The cashier starts tapping on her keyboard again, this time angrily. "I'll have to cancel the transaction, sir."

It's the condensation in her tone that unsticks me.

I double tap the side of my cell, take a step toward the man with the dirt marring his strong chin, clinging to the salt and pepper beard on his jaw, his cheeks. I slip between his strong, obviously hardworking body and the payment kiosk, avoiding those bright blue eyes as I say, "I've got it."

That brilliant cerulean gaze comes to mine. "No, that's—"

But I'm already waving my phone at the machine, and it doesn't so much as have to make contact to solve this problem.

Bleep-beep.

And it's done.

"There," I say softly, giving him a small smile. "Enjoy your meal."

His expression...

Well, I'm not sure I can discern the flurry of emotions—annoyance and surprise and embarrassment and...

Gratitude.

"Thank you," he says softly, snagging the sandwich, soda, and bag of chips from the counter.

"No worries," I reply, turning back to the cashier, taking the receipt she passes over.

He waits there for a moment, big body still, eyes on me, so I turn and hold it out to him.

"Did you need this?" I ask, careful to not get lost in his eyes, careful to not notice how handsome he is, all strong muscles and brutal features and those gorgeous blue irises.

"No," he says.

But doesn't move.

Just stares at me like I'm a puzzle to be solved.

And well...no puzzle here.

Just a woman who's barely holding her life together.

"Right, okay." I nibble at the corner of my mouth. "You have a good day."

Another hesitation from the big man next to me.

"You're all paid, *sir*," the cashier snaps as she starts scanning my items. "You can go now."

I see him stiffen out of the corner of my eye, but he doesn't snap back, and...he doesn't linger.

Just gives a slight nod and walks away.

Some part of me is disappointed.

The rest...is relieved.

Beep. Beep. Beep. Beep—

"Wait," I tell the cashier, as she reaches for the bottle of wine. It's a discount brand, but I'll have to do without it after that $23.26. "I'll pass on the wine," I say softly.

Her eyes come to mine and she rolls hers, silently setting it to the side before reaching for the next item.

A block of cheese.

"And that too," I murmur, doing some mental math. "And the bread," I add when she puts that aside, starts to scan.

More eye rolls, but my math proves to be on point because by the time she finishes scanning—minus the cheese and bread and wine—I have enough left in my account to cover everything else.

I click the button on the side of my phone.

Do another wave of my cell, hear that *bleep-beep.*

And ignore the surly cashier as I bag my items, gather up my receipt, and head out of the store.

I'm putting my bags into my trunk when I feel a presence behind me.

I close the lid, spin around, and—

See the man from the store standing there, eyes flashing, body big and broad and giving more than a few *Daddy* vibes.

My heart skips a beat.

Warmth blooms in my belly.

Lower.

He's too old for me.

But my mind is running away with itself anyway.

"Can I help you—?" I begin.

"Come with me," he mutters.

Before I can protest, he wraps his fingers around my arm.

And drags me away from my car.

———

Thank you so much for joining me on this journey with the Gold hockey family. It's been so fun to write this series (and some might say to torture my characters into their happy endings :)). I really appreciate your support in bringing these stories to life and hope they touched you as much as they touched me!

Tiff's story is happening and if you liked that little sneak peak above, I hope you'll be happy to hear that her and Jean-Michel (yup, the billionaire owner of the Oakland Eagles and Rome's future father-in-law) will get their story in, BOTTLES & BLADES.

I gave my last twenty dollars to a billionaire.
Now he wants to keep me...
Read Tiff's story in BOTTLES & BLADES, book 1 in the Eagles Hockey: Oak Ridge Vineyards series now>

Don't miss Pascal's story in GOLDEN. **I've seen her. I've watched her. But...I can't allow myself to have her.**
CLICK HERE TO READ GOLDEN NOW>

And if you're wanting more hockey, don't miss BROKEN LACES, book 1 in the Eagles Hockey series, available now! **He's the captain. I'm the owner's daughter.**

CLICK HERE TO READ BROKEN LACES NOW>

———

Last, if you enjoy my series, considering supporting me on PATREON! Get access to early releases, bonus content, character art, audiobooks, special edition covers, swag, and much more!

CLICK HERE TO SUPPORT ME>

———

Hate missing Elise's new releases? Love contests, exclusive excerpts and giveaways?

Then signup for Elise's newsletter here!

www.elisefaber.com/newsletter

———

And join Elise's fan group, the Fabinators (https://www.facebook.com/groups/fabinators) for insider information, sneak peaks at new releases, and fun freebies! Hope to see you there!

———

I so appreciate your help in spreading the word about my books, including sharing with friends! Please leave a review on your favorite book site!

GOLD HOCKEY SERIES

Golden
Scored

ALSO BY ELISE FABER

Boldly

Breathless

Ballsy

Bewitched

Blowout

Breathe

A Breakers Christmas

Blazed

Bound

Sierra Hockey Series

Over the Line

Caught from Behind

On the Fly

The Big Skate

Eagles Hockey Series (all stand alone)

Broken Laces

Knotted Laces

Lace 'em Up

Eagles Hockey: Oak Ridge Vineyards

(all stand alone)

Bottles & Blades

Rush Hockey Trilogy #1

Big Puck Energy

Filthy Puckboy

So Pucking Over It

Bad Billionaire's Quickies

Love, Action, Camera (all stand alone)
Dotted Line

Action Shot

Close-Up

End Scene

Meet Cute

Love After Midnight (all stand alone)
Rum And Notes

Virgin Daiquiri

On The Rocks

Sex On The Seats

Life Sucks Series
Train Wreck

Hot Mess

Dumpster Fire

Clusterf*@k

FUBAR

Perfect Storm

Free Fall

Lost Cause

Roosevelt Ranch Series (all stand alone, series complete)
Disaster at Roosevelt Ranch

Heartbreak at Roosevelt Ranch

Collision at Roosevelt Ranch

Regret at Roosevelt Ranch

Desire at Roosevelt Ranch

Phoenix Series (read in order)

Phoenix Rising

Dark Phoenix

Phoenix Freed

Phoenix: LexTal Chronicles (rereleasing soon, stand alone, Phoenix world)

From Ashes

In Flames

To Smoke

KTS Series (all stand alone, series complete)

Riding The Edge

Crossing The Line

Leveling The Field

Scorching The Earth

Cocky Heroes World

Tattooed Troublemaker

ABOUT THE AUTHOR

USA Today bestselling author, Elise Faber, loves chocolate, Star Wars, Harry Potter, and hockey (the order depending on the day and how well her team -- the Sharks! -- are playing). She and her husband also play as much hockey as they can squeeze into their schedules, so much so that their typical date night is spent on the ice. Elise is the mom to two exuberant boys and lives in Northern California. Connect with her in her Facebook group, the Fabinators or find more information about her books at www.elisefaber.com.

- facebook.com/elisefaberauthor
- amazon.com/author/elisefaber
- bookbub.com/profile/elise-faber
- instagram.com/elisefaber
- tiktok.com/@elisefaberauthor
- goodreads.com/elisefaber